SINFULLY MINE

The Five Deadly Sins
Book 3

Kathleen Ayers

© Copyright 2023 by Kathleen Ayers
Text by Kathleen Ayers
Cover by Dar Albert

Dragonblade Publishing, Inc. is an imprint of Kathryn Le Veque Novels, Inc.
P.O. Box 23
Moreno Valley, CA 92556
ceo@dragonbladepublishing.com

Produced in the United States of America

First Edition November 2023
Print Edition

Reproduction of any kind except where it pertains to short quotes in relation to advertising or promotion is strictly prohibited.

All Rights Reserved.

The characters and events portrayed in this book are fictitious. Any similarity to real persons, living or dead, is purely coincidental and not intended by the author.

ARE YOU SIGNED UP FOR DRAGONBLADE'S BLOG?

You'll get the latest news and information on exclusive giveaways, exclusive excerpts, coming releases, sales, free books, cover reveals and more.

Check out our complete list of authors, too!

No spam, no junk. That's a promise!

Sign Up Here

www.dragonbladepublishing.com

―――

Dearest Reader;

Thank you for your support of a small press. At Dragonblade Publishing, we strive to bring you the highest quality Historical Romance from some of the best authors in the business. Without your support, there is no 'us', so we sincerely hope you adore these stories and find some new favorite authors along the way.

Happy Reading!

CEO, Dragonblade Publishing

Additional Dragonblade books by Author Kathleen Ayers

The Five Deadly Sins Series
Sinfully Wed (Book 1)
Sinfully Tempted (Book 2)
Sinfully Mine (Book 3)

The Arrogant Earls Series
Forgetting the Earl (Book 1)
Chasing the Earl (Book 2)
Enticing the Earl (Book 3)
The Haunting of Rose Abbey (Novella)

Chapter One

Andrew Sinclair looked around his room at Emerson House, dismayed at having to leave such comfortable accommodations when he was just growing used to them. The heavy crimson curtains allowed just the right amount of light to shine through the windows overlooking Bruton Street. The jewel tones of the coverlet and walls complimented the curtains and created a peaceful sanctuary for Drew and his thoughts. There was little else to do but depart London for River Crest, the country estate of the Earl of Emerson, his brother, and once Drew's childhood home. His trunks had already been taken downstairs to be loaded onto the coach where Drew's two sisters, Tamsin and Aurora, along with Miss Maplehurst, awaited him.

As a general rule, Drew didn't care for the country. There was no need to wander about woodland paths and fields when there was a perfectly good park in London.

He smoothed down the snowy white of his cravat, nodding in approval at the well-dressed, attractive gentleman staring back in the oval of the mirror. Not a strand of hair out of place. Coat and trousers perfectly tailored. Boots gleaming from a fresh shine. Drew would offer praise to his valet for his appearance if he possessed one. Which he did not. Nor had he ever. Valets were a luxury, along with cooks, maids, grooms, and butlers.

Dunnings had none of those things. The house barely possessed a roof and working fireplaces.

But the fortunes of the Sinclair family had once more changed, this time for the better. This house, the London residence of the Earl of Emerson and his family, was only a few steps from Grosvenor Square. A full staff was in place. A most excellent cook, named Mrs. Cherry, and an enormous butler who went by the name of Holly.

But Drew could sometimes still catch the scent of cabbage and desperation. The smell of Dunnings was rooted in his nostrils and refused to leave. Animals had burrowed into the house surrounded by hedges so thick and overgrown one risked being sliced by getting too close. Birds had roosted in the eaves leaving their droppings. A once sweeping lawn had been left to grow wild with nothing but a chipped fountain, water green and filled with sludge to give an indication it had once been a stately garden.

He had attended dozens of house parties, almost all of which were held in the English countryside, but had rarely ventured further than the tables where whist, piquet, or vingt-un were being played inside. Drew never made it past the terrace in such instances. He wasn't in attendance at such events for the fresh air, sunshine, and annoying rodents scurrying up the trees. Dunnings had ruined the country for him. The constant round of card games and seduction of women was the only escape from the life foisted upon him at Dunnings, plus the purses he won from the overindulged gentry had helped put food on the scarred, wooden table of that crumbling estate he and his siblings had been banished to by Bentley.

Bentley.

The previous Earl of Emerson and the absolute worst older half-brother anyone should have to tolerate. Shortly after inheriting, Bentley embarked on a lavish lifestyle, eventually bankrupting the estate before finally doing his half-siblings a favor and breaking his neck. Even Drew knew better than to race a barouche through the busy streets of London. Drew's brother, Jordan, was now earl.

Which meant the Sinclairs had all returned to London, excepting

Malcolm. He wasn't really sure precisely *where* his twin was at the moment. Somewhere on the Continent.

The day they'd buried Drew's father. The very second Bentley inherited the title, he'd banished the entire family to Dunnings, a long-forgotten estate so far from London by rights it should have been in Scotland but was actually in Northumberland. Forced to exist on Bentley's dubious charity, their existence had been one of hardship and struggle.

Mother died, wasting away into the gray of Dunnings.

His fingers grew stiff as he flicked a loose thread from the sleeve of his coat.

The dust of that place felt as if it were clogging his throat. Drew could almost hear the mice running behind the walls mixing with the sounds of his mother's endless coughing.

Never again.

The Deadly Sins, as London society liked to refer to the Sinclairs, were firmly ensconced once more on Bruton Street. Yes, Bentley had bankrupted the estate, but in an odd touch of irony, coal had been found beneath the barren ground of Dunnings. A great bloody deal of it. London would have to stiffen its upper lip. The Deadly Sins weren't about to be forced from their home again.

Drew now preferred London, though when his father was alive, they'd all lived at River Crest. Odessa, Jordan's recently acquired wife, was slowly restoring the lovely manor house to its previous glory after Bentley had stripped the estate and allowed it to rot. Drew looked forward to seeing River Crest again, though it was filled with ghosts.

"But I can't tup widows and play cards every night for the rest of my life." Drew's purpose in life or rather, the lack of it now that his family's fortunes were once more secure, had gnawed at him as of late. Besides the tupping of agreeable women, which he excelled at, Drew's other talents were more closely related to cards, calculating odds and wagers. He was good with sums, percentages, profits, and the like. A close acquaintance, Charles Worthington, had broached the subject of forming a partnership, one built on investing in various interests for a variety of wealthy gentlemen. The idea of actually having a purpose in life appealed to Drew now that he wasn't in a constant struggle to survive. Something more important than cards and women to occupy his time. He no longer wanted to hop from house party to some other frivolous amusement. The only sticking point was that Drew needed sufficient funds, a stake, for the partnership. Pride kept him from asking Jordan, who was only now climbing out of the hole Bentley had dug for them all, for the money. The money from Dunnings must first take care of the family and the estate.

And Drew wanted to prove he could do this on his own.

"Drew," Tamsin bellowed up the stairs in a wholly unladylike manner. "Hurry along. We are going to be late."

"A moment." Mother would be everywhere at River Crest. He could still see Malcolm, chasing him through the flowers as Mother ran after them, laughing for them to stop. She'd loved wildflowers. Bluebells, daisies, and foxgloves. Nothing too tame for Lady Emerson.

Drew pressed a palm to his heart as he often did when thinking of his brave, inventive mother. Sarah Fitzsimmons had been an actress before becoming the mistress of the married Earl of Emerson. The blackest of marks against the Sinclairs, the fact that Father had wed his mistress and elevated her to countess after the death of his first wife. Bentley had bitterly resented Mother though she did everything in her power to make him a part of the family. She deserved better from him than to be shipped off to Northumberland and eventually die at a shabby, run-down estate.

The anger, old but still raw, pricked at Drew's chest. It was a wound that never entirely healed, the ache refusing to dull over time. After the bustle of London, most would welcome the bucolic countryside, but all those pastures and serene woodland only reminded Drew of Dunnings.

"You'll make us late," Tamsin yelled up the stairs once more. A thump sounded.

Tamsin was literally stomping her feet in agitation. London hadn't tempered her poor manners in the least. Drew really only had hope for Aurora.

"What were you doing, admiring yourself in the mirror?" Tamsin said as Drew made his way down the stairs. "Honestly, Drew, you aren't at all that handsome."

"There are many ladies who would disagree with your opinion, Tamsin." Drew was a bit of a rake. It wasn't his fault he'd been gifted with a great deal of attractiveness.

"Ugh." Tamsin's displeasure greeted him from the bottom of the stairs. "I cannot believe my brother is little better than a card-playing dandy. What would Malcolm say?"

"Malcolm would be grateful he looks enough like me to draw a lady's eye." Twins they might be, but Drew and his brother looked nothing alike. Drew was lean and athletic, made for London's drawing rooms, while Malcolm was broad and muscular. He'd once been a soldier but now claimed he provided various services for wealthy individuals.

In short, Mal was a mercenary. At least that was the consensus of his siblings.

"He'd say you've become a fop," Drew's beautiful, outlandish sister retorted with a raised brow.

Tamsin resembled their mother so strongly that at times he was struck by the sight of her. She was beautiful. Fierce. Overprotective to a fault.

And somehow involved with the Duke of Ware.

Drew toyed with the idea of broaching the subject of Ware during the journey to River Crest, because he wasn't sure what the bloody hell was going on. Tamsin and Ware were pretending an attachment of sorts all because a moth had landed on Tamsin's knee at a ball. Lady

Longwood as well as half the guests had witnessed the incident which necessitated the farce. Tamsin's reputation would not be destroyed and Ware wouldn't have to be honorable.

At least, that is what Miss Maplehurst explained to Drew, frustrated when he didn't grasp the concept of the *vague* attachment.

That must be why Tamsin had rushed into the house the other day, cheeks flushed, lips swollen, absolutely furious and looking like a woman who'd been kissed senseless.

Vague attachment indeed.

Aurora stood beside Tamsin, yawning at Drew's approach. His youngest sister was not an early riser, at least not since arriving in London. Miss Maplehurst was facing the door, watching as a young, muscular Emerson footman rushed to secure a trunk on top of the waiting carriage.

Miss Maplehurst was probably not the best choice of chaperone for Aurora.

"I don't even have time for toast?" he asked, knowing what Tamsin's answer would be.

"No," his sister replied. "We'll miss the train. Mrs. Cherry has packed us a basket. You can dig in there once we get moving." She turned, shepherding Aurora and Miss Maplehurst to the coach.

"Mr. Sinclair." Holly, the Sinclairs' mastiff of a butler, slid around Miss Maplehurst to address Drew. "This arrived for you a short time ago." A fat envelope with Drew's name scrawled across the top with Dunnings just beneath, was in one hand. "I knew you were making preparations for your departure and didn't wish to interrupt."

"Hmm. Thank you, Holly." Drew took the travel-stained packet. "Must have gone to Northumberland first before coming to London. Strange." He couldn't imagine who would have sent him anything at Dunnings because Drew rarely mentioned that he lived at the impoverished estate. And now that the Sinclairs were once more in residence on Bruton Street, Drew *never* mentioned Dunnings to his circle of London friends save Worthington.

Curious.

Holly bowed and moved down the hall, ushering orders to the servants as the family made ready to depart.

Aurora, Miss Maplehurst and Tamsin were all handed into the carriage while Drew halted on the steps and opened the letter. Lines of elegant handwriting met his gaze as he scanned over the words, making sure he understood.

A man named Joshua Black had died and bequeathed the property known as Blackbird Heath in Lincolnshire, to Mr. Andrew Sinclair.

Joshua Black?

Drew wracked his brain for an acquaintance by that name. Finally, the dim recollection of an older gentleman with watery eyes and a terrible, hacking cough came to mind.

Lady Stanhope's house party in Essex.

Joshua Black had been one of the guests along with Drew. Mr. Black had wandered about, often deep in his cups, scouting about for a game of cards. The final evening of the house party, Black lost his entire purse to Drew due to bad luck, but not poor playing. It had been evident to Drew during their brief acquaintance that gambling was a way of life for Black. The way he held the cards in his hands and the blank, shuttered expression on his features while he played told Drew that Black was far from a novice. Only the terrible fits of coughing had interrupted the older man's concentration. When Black lost the last of his coin, Drew tried to leave the table, but Black insisted on one more hand. A chance, he said, to win back all he'd lost.

Blackbird Heath is my estate, little more than a glorified farm, Sinclair. But suitable, I think, for the wager.

Drew had tried to refuse. Black was obviously unwell. The coughing and the flecks of blood on the older man's handkerchief made Drew increasingly uncomfortable, reminding him of his mother's death, dying in a bed not her own at Dunnings. Drew wasn't the most upstanding gentleman. He made his living with cards and sometimes dice. But there were some lines Drew refused to cross. Taking the home of a man who was clearly dying was one.

Black insisted, demanding that Drew, as a gentleman, give him the opportunity to win back his purse.

Drew agreed but intentionally played poorly. Everything he'd spent the night winning from Black he returned with each hand of cards. Black's condition continued to worsen and when the last hand was finished, Drew had excused himself and retired for the evening. He departed the house party the following day, promptly forgetting about Joshua Black.

Drew scanned the letter once more. "Holly," he said. "Please send for Mr. Patchahoo and have my trunks unloaded from the coach. An urgent matter requires my attention. I won't be traveling to River Crest with my sisters at present that will keep me in London for a few more days."

An estate in the country. Or rather, a farm.

Dunnings had once been a farm, before someone realized nothing would grow in that barren place.

Disgust filled him for rolling hills, the filth of animals and cabbage.

Especially the cabbage.

Why couldn't Black have left him a house in London? That would have been useful. Lincolnshire, where this Blackbird Heath was located, wasn't a place Drew found the least appealing. Making his way out to the coach, Drew stuck his head through its open door.

Tamsin promptly swatted him on the arm. "Hurry up. Did you have to check the knot of your cravat once more before venturing out?"

"I like to be presentable and I'm not going to River Crest."

Three pairs of eyes turned to him in surprise.

"An urgent business matter has arisen rather unexpectedly but one which requires my immediate attention. I'll be along in a few days." He flashed a smile at Tamsin, praying she wouldn't protest too much.

"That doesn't work on me, only widows of a certain age," she countered. "Your business interests consist of faro and whist. Rarely anything of importance."

"Untrue. Worth and I are considering a potential partnership."

"Worth." Tamsin rolled her eyes. "He's cut from the same cloth as you. Faro, whist and widows. The more unhappily wed the better. You and Worth will make quite an impression." Tamsin wasn't terribly fond of Worth, finding him to have more rakish inclinations than Drew. "What will I tell Jordan? That a game of cards with Worth kept you from going home to River Crest?"

Why must Tamsin always be so bloody difficult? "You will tell Jordan that an urgent matter arose I needed to see to personally." Namely, the sale of Blackbird Heath. Depending on the condition of the estate or farm, the proceeds should be enough to start his partnership with Worth. He could avoid completely having to go to Jordan for the sum.

Though if Blackbird Heath was anything like Dunnings, Drew's dream might well be doomed.

"But—"

Drew stepped back from Tamsin, nodding in approval as his trunks were once more sitting on the steps of Emerson House. "I promise, I'll join you within a few days. Jordan will understand."

"Drew," she said, lowering her voice. "River Crest is not Dunnings."

"Safe travels." He hopped back up the steps, refusing to acknowledge her remark. Tamsin knew him far too well. Waving until the carriage turned the corner, Drew returned inside and stepped into the drawing room. A whisky was in order while he waited on the arrival of Patchahoo, the Sinclair family solicitor.

Black had described Blackbird Heath as no more than a glorified farm and didn't seem overly attached to his home. The property could well be in a state of disrepair. But much like Dunnings, there might be wealth hidden beneath the barren soil. Minerals of some sort. Coal had been found at Dunnings, after all. Certainly, if the state of Blackbird Heath was poor, it would be worth investigating.

Chapter Two

Patchahoo arrived at Emerson House less than an hour later, dressed in his usual somber attire of crisply tailored coat and trousers. Wise beyond his years, employing Patchahoo was the only good decision Bentley ever made as Lord Emerson. The solicitor was intelligent, detailed, and fiercely loyal to the Sinclair family.

"Mr. Sinclair." Patchahoo bowed slightly. "I came as soon as I could."

"Stop that, Patchahoo. Addressing me so formally. Either call me Sinclair or Drew, I don't care which, but you've sat across the dinner table from me more often than not. You're a member of the Sinclair family, though I well understand why you wouldn't want to go around telling anyone in London."

A chuckle left Patchahoo. "As you wish, Sinclair. If you don't mind, I'll have one of those myself." He nodded towards the whiskey in Drew's hand. "Bushmills?"

"A Sinclair favorite as you well know. Help yourself." Drew gave a wave.

"I assumed you would be on your way to River Crest. Weren't you scheduled to leave today?" Patchahoo crossed the room and made his way to the sideboard, poured a glass of whiskey, then returned to take a chair across from Drew.

"Fate." Drew tossed the envelope on the table between them. "Intervened. I'll follow my sisters in a few days. Depending."

"Very mysterious." Patchahoo reached for the envelope. "May I?"

"Please. It is why I asked you to come."

Patchahoo opened the letter and scanned the contents before putting it aside. There were additional documents, full of legal wording that Drew hadn't bothered to read. Those pages, Patchhoo paid a great deal more attention to.

"Interesting. You've been bequeathed an estate in Lincolnshire." Patchahoo looked up.

"I ascertained as much after reading the letter from Black's solicitor," Drew replied.

"There is a discrepancy in the dates." Patchahoo held up the letter along with the other documents. "Mr. Godwick, Black's solicitor, waited some time before choosing to notify you of your good fortune." The solicitor's brows drew together. "If I read this correctly, Mr. Black died some time ago."

"I assume that is why the letter went to Dunnings first." Drew's stomach soured at the mere mention of the place he'd once lived. "Though how Joshua Black would have known to find me there I don't know. I have no recollection of telling him where I was from. I rarely speak of Dunnings and especially not to a man I'd only just met."

"Even so, it doesn't appear Godwick tried very hard to find you. Pure luck brought this letter to Emerson House. I suppose the land manager in place at Dunnings must have had it forwarded. Or one of the surveyors. Godwick did Black a disservice in not honoring his client's wishes in a more timely manner."

"I don't care if Godwick was the laziest solicitor in all of England and ate a plate of biscuits before informing me. I would like to sell the estate. Blackbird Heath."

"More a farm, according to these papers."

Drew lifted his glass. "Very well, *farm*. I don't care what you wish to call it, Patchahoo. Sell Blackbird Heath for me and get a good price." This was a sign. Drew was convinced of it. He was meant to partner with Worth in the financial sector. Blackbird Heath would be his stake in the enterprise. Worth hadn't demanded he invest a sum in their venture and had even offered to form the partnership without Drew putting forth his own stake, but that didn't sit well.

"The estate is in Lincolnshire, just outside Horncastle." The solicitor flipped through the contents of the envelope, a curious look on his face. "Unfortunately, I can't sell Blackbird Heath for you. No one can."

"Well, why not?" Drew rose to refill his glass. "Black must have an heir, a son or nephew who is disputing the will." His fingers paused on the whiskey.

"Actually, no. Black had no heirs." Patchahoo nodded to the document. "You really didn't read this?"

"I did not," Drew admitted. "And if there is no heir, I don't understand the problem."

"Well, there *is* a Mrs. Black."

"Mrs. Black? Odd, he never mentioned a wife." A vision of an elderly, hunched woman in widow's weeds flashed before Drew. "I'll assume she's as ancient as her late husband."

"Very likely," Patchahoo said. "Her existence may explain the delay in Godwick locating you. Trying to assist the grieving widow who is likely stricken by the fact Black left her home to a complete stranger. Why would he leave Blackbird Heath to you?"

"I intentionally lost it in a wager several years ago." Drew shrugged. "Black and I were playing cards at a house party. I won his entire purse after a few hours and wished to leave it at that, but Black insisted he be given the chance to win back his coin. He offered up Blackbird Heath. I intentionally lost the remaining hands and allowed him to win his purse back. Black coughed and gasped for air the entire time we played. He was obviously ill. I thought I did a better job of appearing to lose."

"He must have guessed. You did him a kindness in not taking his home."

Drew peered into his glass. "My mother didn't have the chance to die in her own bed at River Crest. I couldn't allow that to happen to someone else, even an idiotic, elderly gambler like Black who should have known better. I suppose I can't allow his widow to be homeless either."

"Well, she isn't homeless, actually." Patchahoo regarded him. "There is a stipulation to your ownership of Blackbeard Heath. Mrs. Black is to be allowed to live at the property until she sees fit to depart."

He fell back in his chair. "Is that a nice way of saying she can stay in residence until she dies? Why not just leave the entire estate to her? Never mind." Drew held up a hand. "Now I'm stuck with an elderly widow in addition to a farm in Lincolnshire, neither of which I want." He was beginning to wish that Godwick's letter had never found him.

"Blackbird Heath should be mildly prosperous," Patchahoo said. "Lincolnshire is nothing but acres of barley, wheat, sugar beets, and cabbage. Sheep as well. You could take up farming. Hire a land manager. I can recommend someone if you like."

"Don't speak of cabbage around me, Patchahoo. You are aware of my feelings on that particular vegetable." Cabbage had been the only thing capable of growing at Dunnings and a staple of the Sinclairs' diet for many years. "I don't like the country, as you are aware, and thus don't care to own property with sheep floating about. Besides, I have plans for the proceeds of the sale of Blackbird Heath."

"Your aspirations will have to be placed on hold. At least for now." Patchahoo shuffled the papers, reading over the same paragraph again. "The will is ironclad. Mrs. Black remains."

"So, I must rid myself of Mrs. Black." How difficult could it possibly be?

"You do if you mean to sell Blackbird Heath."

"I wouldn't be tossing her out of her home if I gave her another, correct? I can't remove her forcibly but if I offered her another place to live and she accepted, that would work."

"Yes. They won't prohibit you doing so. A cottage by the sea, perhaps? Or you could offer her a lump sum from the proceeds of the sale. If she's elderly with no children, managing Blackbird Heath on her own might be difficult. I think Godwick was trying to provide Mrs. Black some time by not informing you immediately. She might be grateful for your offer."

Drew nodded slowly. "Agreed. I'll present her with a generous proposal, one contingent upon the sale of Blackbird Heath."

"It will involve a trip to Lincolnshire," Patchahoo reminded him. "Would you prefer I go?"

Drew set down his glass. As much as he despised the thought of barley fields and cows, it should be he, and not Patchahoo who visited Mrs. Black. "No, I'll go."

"I'll prepare a document for the widow to sign, one which gives her a percentage of the sale of the property rather than naming the sum. Since we've no idea what price Blackbird Heath would bring, that seems fair. Hopefully she'll agree."

Drew swallowed his whiskey. "Don't worry, Patchahoo. She'll accept." He smiled at his solicitor. "You forget, widows adore me."

CHAPTER THREE

HESTER BLACK PACED back and forth across the floor of the study, noting the threadbare condition of the rug beneath her feet. Nearly every rug at Blackbird Heath, as well as the furniture, looked just as worn. The house had once been adorned with luxurious rugs and damask covered settees, far too lavish for a farm masquerading as an estate. But while her late husband liked to surround himself with such frivolous décor, he also, rather unfortunately, adored cards and dice far more. There had once been a fine Persian rug decorating the parlor, but that had been sold early in her marriage after Joshua lost at piquet. The fine pair of chairs and the settee covered in blue damask had been sold as well. All that was before Hester realized that they would starve if she didn't take Blackbird Heath in hand. Over the years, she had managed to keep the farm prosperous despite her elderly husband's propensity to gamble.

Damn Joshua.

Their marriage had not been a love match. Far from it. More a marriage of desperation. Still, Hester had thought Joshua bore her some affection. At least enough to keep him from wagering Blackbird Heath on the turn of a card. How wrong she'd been. Worse, Joshua neglected to tell her what he'd done before his death.

Hester paced back across the study once more, uttering every terrible curse she knew at her husband. She seemed unable to escape gambling wastrels. Raised by one, married to another, now she was to be at the mercy of yet a third. There wasn't any doubt that this Andrew Sinclair was cut from the same cloth as Joshua given what she knew. Just another gentleman who made his living by stealing the hard work of others.

When Martin Godwick, her husband's solicitor, informed Hester of the terms of Joshua's will, she'd swooned, clinging to the edge of the desk in her solicitor's office. Martin had assured Hester he would do everything in his power to ensure Sinclair would set foot in Blackbird Heath. After nearly two years with no sign of Andrew Sinclair, Hester had started to breathe easier. She'd allowed herself to become complacent. Perhaps Sinclair, she'd reasoned, as most gamblers did, had come to a bad end. Or Martin would eventually find a way to overturn Joshua's will and she need not be concerned with Sinclair again.

Today, those hopes were coming to an end.

"I am not about to allow some wastrel from London to sell my home," Hester hissed out to the room. A tiny smile lifted the corners of her mouth. "And he can't. Not as long as I am still here." What Joshua had thought to accomplish by adding that condition to his will, Hester had no clue. She only meant Sinclair couldn't throw her out.

Hester moved to stand beside the window, lifting the edge of the curtain to see a well sprung, plain black carriage headed towards Blackbird Heath.

Sinclair.

Hester had formed her own impression of Andrew Sinclair; after all, he'd made her husband's acquaintance over a game of cards. Younger than Joshua. Toothy grin. Well-dressed, of course. Charming in the way most charlatans were. There wasn't any doubt he'd want to sell Blackbird Heath so that he could wager the proceeds on the horses at Newmarket. Or play hazard at one of London's gaming hells. Men of Andrew Sinclair's ilk liked expensive women and brandy. Indulgent living. Wagers on ridiculous things such as the color of a lady's petticoat.

Hester's father had done so once, wagered on the color of a doxy's underthings. It cost Hester what was left of her mother's chest of books, all sold to pay his debt.

Panic hammered in her chest at the thought of Blackbird Heath being sold. Of being reduced once more to eking out the barest sort of existence.

The carriage rolled to a stop outside the front door. There was only one small trunk strapped to the top, that at least was a good sign that Sinclair didn't intend to take up residence. Hopefully, Hester might only have to tolerate him for one night. Or he might choose to stay in Horncastle.

Hester smoothed her features, tucking in a stray strand of auburn hair behind one ear. She must not allow her disgust for Sinclair to show, or her anger over the situation, not if her plan was to succeed. Sinclair *owned* Blackbird Heath, but he couldn't force her out or sell the estate.

Joshua's will was very clear.

Hester planned to impress upon Sinclair the benefit of leaving her as land manager of Blackbird Heath. He would have a steady stream of funds, something no gambler wanted to be without, and never trouble himself with her or the farm. It was much the same relationship Hester had with Joshua. Her husband had wanted to sell off Blackbird Heath, but she'd convinced Joshua otherwise. Her husband had certainly no interest in cabbage, turnips, sugar beets, and sheep, but he did like the profits that came from the fields. So would Sinclair. If he disagreed, Hester would dig in. Eventually, Sinclair would be made to see reason.

It made perfect sense.

The sound of the front door opening and her housekeeper's restrained greeting to Mr. Sinclair echoed down the hall. Mrs. Ebersole dreaded Sinclair's arrival nearly as much as Hester.

She hurried to sit in one of the chairs before the fire, placing her hand over a tear in the fabric covering the chair's arm. Blackbird Heath was profitable, much more so now that Joshua wasn't taking every last farthing to participate in a game of cards, but she had little left over for new chairs or a rug. Animals needed feed. Fertilizer, seeds, plows. Hester had recently cleared another acre which had fallen into disuse. Potatoes were in the ground. Her hard work, her efforts would produce results.

She placed her hands in her lap, frowning at the reddened, rough skin and hid her fingers in the folds of her skirts. Struggling to compose herself, Hester straightened her spine and faced the door.

Blackbird Heath was the first real home she'd ever had. Wedding Joshua at twenty had been more because her father offered up her hand in lieu of the repayment of a debt than anything else. Desperate to escape her circumstances, Hester had agreed to the match. Marriage meant food and a roof over her head, not being evicted from one cottage or room after another and begging for scraps. She'd embraced Blackbird Heath, feeling as if she could breathe for the first time in her life.

Now Joshua had made Hester a guest in her own home.

"Damn you, Joshua Black. I'll say no more prayers for your salvation."

Joshua had made no provisions for Hester. No money. No trinkets she could sell. Certainly, not Blackbird Heath.

The heavy tread of a man's footsteps sounded in the foyer, along with the click of Mrs. Ebersole's heels.

Hester sunk her fingers further into the fabric of her skirts, nail catching on a tiny hole in the muslin. She and her wardrobe were very much like the chair in which she sat. In dire need of repair. This dress was one of her best, though old, and far out of fashion. Hester rarely spent money on anything other than Blackbird Heath.

A sharp rap sounded on the study door.

Hester lifted her chin, politely defiant. Sinclair could not evict her.

The door swung open. "Mr. Sinclair to see you, missus." Mrs. Ebersole's mannish form waved Hester's nemesis in without further preamble, homely features contorted into disapproval. Her housekeeper had the face of a bulldog and the loyalty to match. Blackbird Heath was also Mrs. Ebersole's home.

Hester exchanged glances with the housekeeper as Sinclair stepped into the study.

Sunlight streamed through the window behind Hester, keeping her in shadow while near blinding him. He blinked, unable to see her clearly, which was intentional on her part. She'd wanted a moment to take Sinclair's measure before he tried to take ownership of Blackbird Heath.

"Thank you, Mrs. Ebersole." Hester tilted her chin, observing the tall, lean gentleman before her.

Hester's pulse skipped twice before settling.

Handsome. Hester would give Sinclair that much. Far younger than she'd imagined him to be. Well-dressed, which she'd expected for a gentleman of his pursuits. Joshua had always possessed a fine wardrobe. Sinclair's cravat was snowy white and perfectly twisted but absent of ornamentation. Not that Sinclair required additional adornment, not a man of his magnificence.

A rake of the first order.

The mossy green of his eyes, flashing like emeralds as the light slid across his sculpted features, widened at the sight of her. A brilliant, disarming smile pulled at the sensual mouth in greeting, one she assumed Sinclair used often and to great effect.

Hester was not immune. Her heart fluttered once more, though dislike of him threatened to spill out of her.

"Mrs. Black, I presume."

"Mr. Sinclair." Her tone was crisp and polite.

He took a step closer, and Hester caught the scent of cedar and leather hovering around his broad shoulders. Sinclair's movements were smooth. Practiced. Casually strutting across her study like a barnyard cat looking for a spot in the sun, but much more overtly carnal in nature. Used to drawing the gaze of any woman with whom he crossed paths. He did everything but pose before Hester in all his masculine glory. How many skirts had been lifted with just a wink from those mossy green eyes?

Hester was not impressed. Yes, Sinclair was glorious, but she knew what lay beneath that handsome interior. The overindulgence of a pampered existence. Her hands were likely rougher than his.

"Now that we have those introductions out of the way." Sinclair slid into the chair across from Hester, stretching out his legs and crossing them at the ankle. The fabric of his trousers pulled at the muscles of his thighs, once more drawing her eye without Hester's permission.

The barest prickling rippled along her skin, the awareness of the large, attractive man just across from her. Unexpected and unwanted. More annoyance than anything else.

She quickly jerked her gaze away.

He was nothing more than a practiced flirt possessed of a charming manner. A manner that was meant to lure Hester into complacency so that he could rip out Blackbird Heath from beneath her.

What arrogance.

"I trust your journey from London was without incident, Mr. Sinclair."

As if on cue, the maid, Mary, arrived with a tea tray. She bobbed politely, tried not to stare at Sinclair, who frankly, was well worth staring at though Hester hated to admit to it, then bustled out.

"Pleasant enough." Sinclair agreed in his posh London accent. Another reason to dislike him. She found those from London spoke with a high degree of snobbishness. "I confess, Mrs. Black, I'm surprised. I expected you to be…more Mr. Black's contemporary."

A nice way of saying Sinclair had hoped Hester would be a woman of advanced years that he could conveniently ship elsewhere while he stripped Blackbird Heath and sold it.

Her hands curled into fists before she relaxed once more.

"I'm sorry to have disappointed you, Mr. Sinclair." Pouring out two cups of tea, Hester tried not to glance at her hands as she placed one before him. She should have worn gloves, but the only pair she possessed with a size too large and meant for physical labor.

"Oh, I didn't say I was disappointed. Only surprised." The discerning green perused her, lingering overly long on Hester's waist and bosom.

Cur.

"You, Mr. Sinclair, are exactly as I expected." Hester stared boldly back at him.

Sinclair's lips twisted into a half-smile, probably wondering why his usual tactics were having little effect on Hester. "I'm not partial to tea, Mrs. Black. Do you have something stronger? Whiskey, perhaps? Anything Irish?"

Of course. Why not spirits? It was barely noon. The true mark of a gentleman who lived for excess. "I believe there is a bottle at the sideboard. I'm uncertain of its provenance. My husband preferred brandy." She made to stand.

Sinclair waved her down. "I'll help myself with your permission."

How polite. Civilized. It was all Hester could do to keep from screaming that he owned everything at Blackbird Heath but her, so why bother to ask. Slowly inhaling through her nose, she willed the anger at her situation to abate. A loss of temper would be disastrous, especially if she wished to reach an agreement with him.

He smiled at her once more as he sauntered over to the sideboard. Hester half expected him to wink at her.

Ugh.

Joshua hadn't stood a chance at defeating Sinclair across a card table, not with all that smug charm and excessive politeness. He'd probably been shocked at losing. Not a hint of the journey from London even showed on Sinclair. No gleam of moisture on his brow, though the day was warm. No dirt on his boots or dust on his coat. He could have just left the ministrations of his valet.

Hester, on the other hand, spent her days covered in sweat and smelling of animals or manure. And she would continue to do so to benefit this card wielding dandy so that Blackbird Heath would survive.

So I will survive.

"Blackbird Heath is a lovely estate," he ventured over his shoulder. "More of a farm, I suppose."

"You seem surprised. Was it the sheep grazing over the rise or the barn that gave it away?" Hester closed her mouth before she could say more. Sarcasm would not get her what she wanted.

Sinclair raised a brow. "Mr. Black gave me the impression that Blackbird Heath, his *estate* which is also a farm," he emphasized, "was of little value."

There it was. The flash of ruthlessness. Greed. A hard edge hiding behind all that masculine beauty.

"My husband did not appreciate Blackbird Heath as I do. He didn't see the value of growing crops or tending sheep. But doing so keeps one well fed. Comfortable."

"I've never cared for the countryside overmuch, Mrs. Black. I prefer London."

Well, that was good. He wouldn't want to stay here long. "My husband did as well." She swallowed. Now was as good a time as any to start the discussion she hoped would have a positive outcome. "As you can imagine, I wasn't pleased to be informed of the change to my husband's will. I did not find out until after his funeral. I should like to put forth a proposal, if I may, Mr. Sinclair."

"A proposal?" Sinclair returned to his seat; a glass of amber colored liquid clutched in one hand. He raised the glass and sniffed, nose wrinkling, but did not take a sip. "That sounds vaguely improper on such short acquaintance."

Sinclair's words had a lazy, seductive quality as if he'd just awoken from a nap and was stretching across the sheets of his bed. Another ripple of sensation wafted along Hester's arms and she struggled to keep from flinging the entire pot of tea in his handsome face. Attraction to a man, especially this man, wasn't something she'd prepared for. It was unsettling.

"My proposal is one of a financial nature, Mr. Sinclair. As you've seen, Blackbird Heath is mostly pasture and fields. More farm than estate, as you've mentioned. We grow potatoes. Sugar Beets. Turnips. Cabbages—"

Sinclair frowned. "I'm not fond of cabbage."

"A great many people are. On the north pasture, sheep. The sort only bred in Lincolnshire with long wool. My herd is small at present but growing. Vastly profitable."

A flicker of interest shone in the eyes. "Pigs?"

Hester took a deep breath. Perhaps they could come to an understanding. "Yes. Pigs. Chickens. The crops are the most profitable part of our enterprise and I've also started producing honey, but the demand for wool will eventually—"

Sinclair held up a hand, stopping her. "I'm sure your animal husbandry is second to none, Mrs. Black. But as I mentioned, I don't care for the country. London is more my preference."

"The proposal I would like to offer you does not require you to reside at Blackbird Heath." She took a deep breath. "I would manage the farm on your behalf. Keep Blackbird Heath profitable. You need not do anything. I would consult you on large expenses, of course." She wouldn't, but Sinclair was highly unlikely to look at the ledgers on a regular basis.

"Of course." He leaned back in his chair, glass clutched in one hand. "I would expect nothing less." The glass raised and he took a sip, grimacing slightly.

"You would have a steady stream of income for your various pursuits," she finished. "I would not bother you except to send you funds. You need never come to Lincolnshire again."

"Why, you make it seem as if I'll be a kept man, Mrs. Black. What sort of pursuits do you think I have?"

"You prefer London; thus, I would assume your interests lie there as well. You seem to be a gentleman much like my husband." Hester had to pause lest too much disdain bleed into her words. "Mr. Black did not care to reside in the country and also required a great deal of income to support his lifestyle. In London."

Sinclair rolled the glass between his hands. "I see."

Hester cleared her throat. "I have been managing Blackbird Heath on my own for years, Mr. Sinclair. I realize this is somewhat unusual, but I am land manager in everything but name. I know what I'm doing."

"That is abundantly clear, Mrs. Black."

"Surely you can see the benefit of allowing things to continue as they are." Sinclair didn't strike her as obtuse, only arrogant. "You would have no responsibility. I wouldn't expect you to assist me with anything."

His elegant fingers drummed along the edge of his glass. "How selfless of you, Mrs. Black. You continue to reside here, milking cows and growing cabbage while I return to London. I must admit that your proposal has merit, though it is highly unconventional."

Hester held her breath for a space, waiting for him to agree. Her fingers returned to her lap to twist about.

"And while I am certain of your talents in regards to Blackbird Heath," Sinclair continued. "I have a counterproposal."

She deflated somewhat into the seat of her chair. Determination stiffened her shoulders.

Sinclair reached inside his pocket and withdrew an envelope. "The sum I would receive from the sale of Blackbird Heath, invested over the next ten years with interest, would far eclipse any income you could derive from this estate. And that is if you could avoid diseased animals, plant blights, or other natural disasters."

Hester refused to back down. "I disagree."

"You are free to do so." He opened the envelope and spread the document before her. "I did my research before arriving here, Mrs. Black. I'm well aware of Blackbird Heath's worth, the success of which is due to your excellent stewardship." A smile flashed at her.

"How kind."

"Upon you vacating Blackbird Heath, I mean to sell the estate or *farm*." Another charming grin. "You would receive a sizable percentage of the sale." He tapped the document. "I've been more than generous. I can take the sum and invest it for you, if you like. You'll be comfortable for the rest of your life. You can travel. See the world. Visit London."

Hester snorted. "Until the right card game comes along, isn't that the case? I'll find my accounts stripped bare and left with nothing. What a kind offer, Mr. Sinclair. But I must decline."

"You think I would take—" The smile fled from his lips. "Fine. You receive the percentage outright and do what you wish with it. I was only involving myself as a courtesy."

"A courtesy would have been not to come here," she snapped, all pretense of being polite dropping at his words.

"The fact remains that *I* own Blackbird Heath, Mrs. Black," he shot back. "No matter how much you may wish I do not. I am not going to disappear simply because you will it."

"More's the pity." Sinclair, like every other man she'd ever known, saw no value in the land or the people, just the bloody coin he could wager in a hand of cards. Blackbird Heath was worth far more than a game of dice. The people here depended on her. This was her home. How dare he reduce it to nothing more than a business transaction.

"I cannot allow you to stay here indefinitely." Anger sharpened his previously polite tone. "In the hopes that I will change my mind or Mr. Godwick will find a way to overturn your husband's will."

"Yet according to my husband's will, Mr. Sinclair, that is exactly what *you* must do." She gave a disgusted sigh. "Go back to London. Find a game of cards to entertain yourself. Indulge in your usual pleasures." Disdain curled her lip. "I'm not leaving Blackbird Heath to your tender care. Nor can you force me to."

Chapter Four

Harridan.
　　One with an incredible mane of auburn hair, but still—
Termagant.

His proposal made perfect sense. Anyone could see it except for the shrew defiantly dismissing him from her parlor. Mrs. Black's percentage from the sale of Blackbird Heath was overly generous. Kind.

Bloody obstinate woman.

Blackbird Heath *was* little more than a glorified farm. As if some minor lord had once built a lovely manor house and decided, after a bit, he'd rather be a country squire. The entire property wasn't designed to be a workable farm. You couldn't even see the barn or other outbuildings from the drive. He was offering Mrs. Black a comfortable living for the remainder of her days, and she wanted to be his land manager.

The idea was absurd.

Mrs. Black was supposed to be an ancient crone with a cap of lace on her head and dressed in widow's weeds, not a strident spitfire with an abundance of copper hair.

Good Lord. Why did she have to be a redhead?

Fortunately, Mrs. Black possessed the personality of a mule, a sparse bosom, from what Drew could see and less than generous curves. All of which was more than enough to quell Drew's initial interest in her.

Yet his cock still twitched in her direction each time she spoke.

The damned red hair was at fault.

Patchahoo, in the limited time he'd been given, had done an excellent job on researching the value of Blackbird Heath, though he'd failed in the assessment of Mrs. Black. The land surrounding the estate was fertile but underutilized. Yes, Mrs. Black had fabulous wooly sheep grazing in the pasture, but the herd wasn't large. She lacked labor and modernization, both of which cost money. So, while Blackbird Heath seemed incredibly prosperous, most of the profits were being driven back into the farm to keep it operating. A large investment would be required to truly expand operations at Blackbird Heath, funds Drew would rather use to form a partnership with Worth, not turn into bloody cabbages and turnips. Or god forbid, a thresher.

Patchahoo had made several discreet inquiries to some of the large landowners in the area, all of whom failed to mention Mrs. Black wasn't an elderly widow. There was a great deal of interest in the town of nearby Horncastle over Blackbird Heath. Joshua Black had been pressured to sell many times, but his wife always dissuaded him. The farm was worth a small fortune, at least to the other landowners in Lincolnshire.

Mrs. Black, fists clenched in her lap, had tilted her chin in his direction, fairly demanding Drew throw her out. She wasn't beautiful. Pretty, maybe. Her nose was not the pert button of so many London beauties, but long and thin. Skin the color of a peach with a wealth of freckles across the bridge. Lithe. No curves, but Drew imagined firmly muscled thighs and calves beneath her skirts.

His cock twitched again.

And redheads usually had freckles in places other than their cheeks.

His lips tightened.

High cheekbones, which gave Mrs. Black's perfectly average deep brown eyes a slight tilt at the ends. Drew's gaze passed once more over her nonexistent décolletage. Unspectacular. Her mouth, though, now *that* was something deserving of further attention when not formed into an unfriendly rosette, as it was at present.

He wondered if she ever smiled and decided Mrs. Black did not.

"It seems we are at an impasse, Mrs. Black."

"That we are, Mr. Sinclair."

"I did you the courtesy of listening to your proposal, but you refuse to even consider mine." Drew drummed his fingers along the glass. He wasn't sure what the glass contained. Not brandy, exactly. Or whiskey.

"Very well. I don't wish to be discourteous." Mrs. Black picked up the document Patchahoo had prepared, scanning over the pages with little interest, before placing them back on the table. "I do not accept your proposal. Mine is far more beneficial to us both."

"Mrs. Black—"

"Let me be blunt, Mr. Sinclair. You cannot forcibly remove me from Blackbird Heath nor can you sell my home unless I leave it, which I have no intention of doing."

According to Patchahoo, that portion of Black's will was set in stone. Blackbird Heath could not be sold unless Mrs. Black *abandoned the property of her own free will*. The wording Black had used was strange, but the meaning was clear. Black had obviously been torn between honoring what he felt was a debt to Drew and the future care of his wife. The older man had probably assumed Drew would give Mrs. Black a lump sum to vacate but hadn't accounted for his wife's stubbornness.

"Did you meet your husband over a game of cards?" Drew said, deftly changing the topic of their conversation, purely to irritate her. Mrs. Black had made her dislike of card playing evident within moments of their introduction. "Or perhaps you thought Black cut a fine figure dancing the jig. Oh, I know." He leaned forward. "You were admiring plow horses and he came upon you."

Pasting a polite smile on her face, she stated crisply, "That is none of your affair." A furious breath strained the fabric of her dress.

The liquid in Drew's glass was overly smoky, which led him to believe it must be whiskey, though the taste was less than appealing. Still better than tea. He took another cautious sip. "I'm merely curious."

"Had you any decency at all, Mr. Sinclair..." Her cheeks flushed beneath her lightly tanned skin. "You would relinquish Blackbird Heath to me."

Mrs. Black turned a lovely shade of pink when she was distressed.

"I thought you had already established my lack of decency, Mrs. Black, upon my arrival." He was doing a poor job of charming this particular widow, something Drew was ordinarily quite good at.

"I knew what sort of gentleman you were after learning you took advantage of an obviously sick and elderly man. Your kindness," she drawled, voice thick with sarcasm, "by not taking his home that night. You merely decided to delay your greed."

Mrs. Black had formed a blistering and incorrect opinion of him. He could have told her about Dunnings. Explained that he knew what it was to have your home taken from you. The irony of this horribly awkward situation wasn't lost on Drew. *Most* gentlemen would have taken everything from Black that night. But his conscience had dictated differently. Now he was stuck with this obstinate redhead who couldn't see that Drew wasn't tossing her aside as much as offering her a comfortable life. What woman in her right mind would choose the backbreaking labor of holding an entire farm together on her own?

Mrs. Black, apparently.

"You've nothing to say in your defense, Mr. Sinclair?" A snort of derision. "I thought not," Holding up Drew's proposal, Mrs. Black ripped the document in half before taking great care to tear it into tiny portions which she then tossed up in the air, smiling at him the entire time.

Drew's cock twitched again. Troublesome organ to be attracted to this harpy.

The bits of paper fluttered down, landing on his arm and in his glass of terrible whiskey. Or whatever was in his glass. The liquid tasted like the ashes of a fire.

Typically, Drew was slow to anger. His older brother, Jordan, and Tamsin, both possessed volatile tempers. Malcolm sometimes behaved like an enraged bull. Drew's role had always been that of peacemaker among the Sinclairs. The charming brother who believed in negotiation and rarely made waves.

But he'd had quite enough of this cantankerous widow. No matter how prettily she blushed.

"It seems no good deed goes unpunished, Mrs. Black. I will tell you that had you not ripped up my offer, I would have done so."

She fell back, the smug smile fading.

"When I sell Blackbird Heath, and I *will*, you will no longer receive a portion of the proceeds. There will be nothing for you. Not a farthing."

"You are not permitted to sell Blackbird Heath while I live here."

"Entirely true." She would leave of her own accord. Mrs. Black just hadn't yet realized the situation she'd put herself in. "May I use pen and paper?" He gestured to the desk with a flick of his wrist. Drew was no stranger to gossip. The Sinclairs, after all, were riddled with scandal.

"If you think to send for your solicitor to have him produce another offer—"

"I've already told you my generosity towards you has been revoked. And I wouldn't dream of having Patchahoo waste any more of his time." He stood and walked over to the desk. "That's my solicitor.

Patchahoo. He's a lovely man. Much kinder than I." Drew heard the slip of his upper-crust accent into the gentle rolling of Northumberland. A sign of his annoyance and mounting anger at this entire situation. Mrs. Black was meant to be a pale old woman made of lace and grief who he could settle a small cottage on.

A gnat landed on his cheek, and he slapped at it.

I hate the bloody country.

Mrs. Black was determined, but Drew was just as resolute. He had survived Dunnings, after all. He meant to take advantage of the opportunity with Worth. And he meant to do it without going to his brother Jordan to do so.

"I'm merely writing my solicitor to have my things sent to Blackbird Heath." He winked at her. "Can you have Mrs. Ebersole prepare a room for me upstairs? I'd be so grateful."

Mrs. Black stood abruptly, pale beneath her freckles, the lovely blush of her anger gone in an instant. "You plan to stay? But that is improper. You cannot—"

"I most certainly can, Mrs. Black. This..." He waved a hand around. "Is my home as much as yours. Of course, my reputation won't suffer a bit, wastrel that I am. Oh, I shouldn't worry about your own. I'm sure you are beloved in Horncastle."

Mrs. Black paled further.

Drew assumed as much.

"I am—an unmarried woman. A widow."

"Who refuses to leave my property though I generously offered her a lump sum to do so. I'm sure there will be speculation. After all..." He held up the pen. "Look at me. Why wouldn't you wish to stay beneath the same roof. It might be my virtue that is in danger. You might have designs on me. Lonely widow and all that."

"You arrogant—"

"If my presence at Blackbird Heath bothers you, feel free to find other accommodations which better suit you. Now, if you'll excuse me, I've got to get off this note to Patchahoo. I've a mind to venture into Horncastle and introduce myself. I'll inform Mrs. Ebersole to prepare a room for me. After all, she is my housekeeper. No need to concern yourself further. I'll see you at dinner."

Drew gave her his back, scratching out the letter to Patchahoo.

A sputtering sound came from behind him. An indignant breath. Finally, the agitated swirl of her skirts and the slamming of the parlor door.

Drew hummed out loud, a ribald tune he was sure Mrs. Black would disapprove of, then finished his letter to Patchahoo.

Chapter Five

Hester entered Blackbird Heath's small dining room, unused since Joshua's death. The room wasn't grand in size, the furniture outdated, but it was a cozy place to have a meal. Hester had been eating in the kitchens because it seemed ridiculous for Mrs. Ebersole to go to the additional effort of serving her here. The lamps had been lit and fresh flowers placed on the table, giving the illusion that Blackbird Heath had once been a moderately grand estate and not the farm it was now.

Mr. Sinclair sat at the head of the table; elegant fingers curled around a glass of wine. Hooded eyes took her in, showing no surprise that Hester's dress was the same she'd greeted him in hours ago. After their contentious meeting in the study, Hester had gone about her chores, only pausing to tie an apron about her waist and put on her boots. Walking the fields and examining the potatoes and turnips had failed to banish Sinclair from her mind. Returning only a short time ago, Hester washed and repined her hair, seeing no reason to primp for the man trying to take her home.

"In the country, we don't change our attire at every hour," she said, just to show her annoyance at his presence. "Nor do I have an army of servants to pour you wine."

Sinclair shrugged, his eyes following her as Hester settled herself. "I think you mean *I* don't have an army of servants."

"I stand corrected, Mr. Sinclair," Hester shot back.

Mrs. Ebersole arrived, pushing a small cart filled with steamed turnips, fresh bread, and a wedge of cheese.

Dobbins, one of Hester's farmhands, scrubbed and in fresh clothing, came behind her carrying a covered tray which was placed on the table with a flourish.

"Thank you, Dobbins," Hester murmured.

"Bubble and Squeak." Mrs. Ebersole grunted, taking the fresh bread and butter from the cart and placing it on the table. "Cheddar." She slapped down the wedge of cheese. Ripping off the lid of the tray, she gave Sinclair a hostile look. "Dinner is served."

Sinclair's lips rippled, nostrils flaring as the aroma of Bubble and Squeak filled the room. "Might there be some roasted chicken, perhaps?"

"No sir. Not tonight," Mrs. Ebersole said. "I already had things well in hand when you informed us you were staying to dine. Apologies. But I can prepare a chicken tomorrow evening, if that suits you."

"Splendid." He was looking at the dish of potatoes, cabbage, and bacon with utter terror.

"Something amiss, Mr. Sinclair? Do you not care for Bubble and Squeak?" Hester inquired politely, taking a sip of her own wine. "This is the country. We dine on simple fare."

"Not at all." He took a spoonful and placed it carefully on his plate, followed by half the loaf of bread and a large piece of cheese.

Hester filled her own plate, noting that Sinclair picked out the potatoes and bacon, and furiously pushed aside the cabbage as if it might attack him. Sinclair truly didn't care for cabbage, it seemed. A pity. Because Hester meant to tell Mrs. Ebersole to serve cabbage at every meal. Maybe she could starve him back to London.

Hester sipped her wine and considered all the things a gentleman from London might not like about the country. Vermin. Cabbages. The crowing of roosters.

"Plotting my demise, Mrs. Black?"

"Not at all, Mr. Sinclair. I was only considering how quiet you'll find the country after living in London."

He shrugged, the moss of his eyes flat and giving no hint to his thoughts as he watched her. "Do you always attack your meals with such relish, Mrs. Black?"

Hester paused in her chewing, taking a swallow of wine. Joshua had often proclaimed her appetite unseemly for a woman. But she worked hard all day, as much as or more than some of her farmhands. And as much as she ate, Hester's frame stayed sparse with few hints of softness. Still, her cheeks reddened in embarrassment before considering that Sinclair had given her another weapon against him.

Hester shoveled more food into her mouth, groaning loudly in pleasure. Drops of grease splattered on her chin.

"Really, Mrs. Black. I've seen feral dogs with better table manners."

"I am hungry. The result of hard work. I doubt you know the feeling."

"Of hunger? I assure you I do." There was an odd glint in his eyes. "And they say we are uncivilized," he muttered under his breath.

Hester put down her fork. "Who?"

A short bark of laughter came from him as he buttered a piece of bread, as gracefully as he did everything else. "You've nothing on my sister, Tamsin."

Chapter Six

Hester awoke the following morning refreshed and full of renewed enthusiasm, her mind spinning with how she might best run Sinclair off. She'd start with food. Before retiring for the night, she'd instructed Mrs. Ebersole that Sinclair *adored* cabbage and wished it to be served at every meal. Even breakfast. He simply could not get enough of it.

Mrs. Ebersole looked dubious, given Sinclair's horror at the Bubble and Squeak, but nonetheless, agreed.

Then Hester found Jake, one of her farmhands, and asked him to move King George closer to the house for the benefit of Mr. Sinclair. Sinclair, she explained, simply adored the sound of a cock crowing to herald the dawn. King George, Hester's cantankerous rooster, was excellent at waking the entire household.

True, King George and cabbage might not force Sinclair to leave, but it was an excellent start. Sinclair needed to depart Blackbird Heath before the good people of Horncastle's opinion of Hester Morton, now Black, became any worse. Hard enough growing up as the daughter of the town sot, a pathetic creature pitied and derided by most of the town, without also becoming known as a harlot.

Donning her oldest dress, apron and boots, Hester set out to walk along the fields as the sun was rising. She'd heard King George greet the dawn, his crow sounding like thunder as near as Jake had put him to the house. Hester had even startled at the sound. When she left

Sinclair last night, he was still nursing a brandy in the front parlor, a book in his lap. Mrs. Ebersole had found him a bottle of brandy stashed in the kitchen. Apparently, what he'd found earlier in sideboard didn't meet his expectations.

Overindulged fop.

It was strange he'd been reading. Hester never considered that gamblers read a great deal. Neither her husband nor father put much stock in the value of books.

She did hope Sinclair hadn't stayed up into the wee hours drinking his brandy, only to be awoken by King George.

Giggling to herself, Hester climbed up the small hill so she could see the morning light filtering over her fields. Pride filled her at the sight of all she'd accomplished. When Joshua had first brought her to Blackbird Heath, Hester had been a determined, desperate girl of twenty, one with only dim recollections of the farm her grandfather once owned. Where Joshua saw the shabbiness of Blackbird Heath, Hester saw a challenge. She'd worked and struggled to make Blackbird Heath a home and had hoped to pass it on to children one day.

A sigh left her.

There was a reason Joshua Black had still been a bachelor at his age. An injury in his youth made physical relations difficult and the possibility of children impossible. The marriage *had* been consummated. Barely. Physical relations were sparse thankfully and after a time Joshua ceased seeking Hester out at all.

She didn't mind. She was more interested in Blackbird Heath.

On more than one occasion, particularly if he had lost a great deal at the most recent house party he attended, Joshua would insist Blackbird Heath needed to be sold. Mr. Scoggins, a large landowner in the vicinity had wanted to purchase Blackbird Heath for some time, but never managed to offer enough to sway Joshua. Especially after she would dutifully trot out the ledgers, pointing out to her husband the profitability of Blackbird Heath.

Wouldn't it be better, Hester would say, to have a steady source of income? A place to return to? If he sold to Scoggins, all of that would be gone.

Joshua, thankfully, hadn't pushed her. He'd taken what he wished for his amusements and left her to run the farm as she saw fit.

Last night, as she lay in bed, listening to the breeze blow through the curtains of her bedroom window, Hester allowed herself to consider what her life would become if she had accepted Sinclair's proposal. No responsibility. She could leave this tiny corner of Lincolnshire and Horncastle with all the bad memories of her childhood and become someone else.

Tempting.

She looked out at the sun gilding her beautiful fields as it rose in the sky.

But what Hester wanted most, the only thing she'd ever cared about, was a place to call her own. Great wealth would never be possible for her. Or influence. Not even love. But she had the land. Animals. Growing things. Those things gave her a sense of purpose. The dirty half-starved child she'd once been, daughter of the town sot who had gambled away every bit of coin he possessed or drank it away. Thomas Morton had been a poor excuse for a father. A wastrel of a man who cared more for a hand of cards than his own flesh and blood. Her childhood was a series of progressively smaller cottages, until Father was reduced to renting them a room in Horncastle above the tavern.

Never again.

She turned and strode resolutely toward the chicken coop. King George must be congratulated on his performance this morning if he was about. Jake had put a large bowl of feed for him just beneath Sinclair's window last night and would do so every night that charlatan was in residence.

Reaching the chickens, Hester went to the barrel containing their feed, tossing out handfuls into the dirt. King George appeared from a spray of bushes, strutting forward and pecking at her skirts.

"Splendid job this morning, Your Majesty," she praised the rooster.

"Set better than a clock," a silky masculine voice said from behind her.

Hester turned slowly to face him. The bane of her existence awake and freshly shaven, clothes neat as a pin. Not looking the least out of sorts.

How incredibly annoying.

Hester had debated putting something lumpy in Sinclair's mattress to ensure his night was as uncomfortable as possible, but decided King George would be enough.

She'd been wrong.

"Mr. Sinclair." Hester kept tossing out the feed. "I didn't expect you up so early."

"Did you not, Mrs. Black? The country is only quiet in the evenings. I fear the mornings are more boisterous. You've named your rooster King George?" He entered the enclosure.

Hester faced him, taking in the expensive boots on his feet. The finely tailored trousers. His trunks with spare clothing would take some time to arrive from London and there was a large pile of chicken dung lying between her and Sinclair.

"I did, Mr. Sinclair. He's quite regal, don't you think? You are free to inspect him," she gently lured Sinclair forward. If he didn't see the dung, it was hardly her fault.

"Is Queen Charlotte about?" He took another step, still not looking down.

"No, but I do have Elizabeth the Eggcellent Egg Layer and Mary Tudor. Mary is a little bitter. She doesn't produce as many eggs." She tried to stop the smile on her face as Sinclair stepped right into the middle of—

"Bloody hell."

The dung, probably King George's leavings, splattered upward, staining the edge of Sinclair's trousers, and coloring his boots.

"Oh, dear." Hester pretended to be horrified. "You should watch where you walk, Mr. Sinclair. This is a farm, after all."

"Yes, the countryside seems littered with unpleasantness." Sinclair looked over at her before going to the small fence and knocking the dung from his boots. Next, he took a handkerchief out of his pocket and wiped off the bottom of his trousers, grimacing the entire time.

Hester pursed her lips. She'd been hoping for curses. A flailing of the arms as he realized certain clothing might well be ruined. Perhaps screeching like a small child.

"I'll just go and clean up, shall I?" Sinclair said in a bemused tone.

※

CONNIVING SHREW.

Drew didn't blame Mrs. Black completely for the dung coloring his trousers and boots. He'd forgotten what it was like to walk through a place where animals roamed about. Mrs. Black hadn't bothered to warn Drew and he'd been too busy watching a strand of copper hair dancing against her cheek to pay attention to where he stepped.

Things would be so much easier if her hair was a muddy shade of brown.

Stretching out his fingers, Drew tossed aside the soiled handkerchief and marched back to the house in search of Mrs. Ebersole, who would surely know how to get dung out of trousers.

Perhaps he shouldn't have commented when they dined that Mrs. Black devoured her supper like one of the starving dock workers in Spittal. Well, fine. She'd had her revenge. It was only that he'd never seen a woman consume so much food in such a short period of time and with such gusto. Smacking her lips and groaning in delight. He could still smell the lingering scent of cabbage in the air.

Beets. Turnips. Carrots. Potatoes. Drew could tolerate any of them. But *never* cabbage.

The smell alone made him want to pinch at his nose.

Thank goodness for the bread and cheese. He'd ended the evening with brandy, reluctantly procured by Mrs. Ebersole. The brandy had nearly erased the aroma of cabbage still clinging to his clothes. He'd waited patiently for Mrs. Black to retire, then boldly made his way to the study, and pulled out a stack of ledgers. He'd fallen asleep atop the desk, exhausted from his journey, cabbage and Mrs. Black.

King George woke him. The rooster seemed to be right outside the window. Upon further inspection, Drew realized the room he'd been given was directly above the study. Odd that the rooster wasn't closer to the hens.

Upon seeing Mrs. Black's surprise at his appearance, not so strange after all.

Taking care to discard his boots outside, Drew went in search of Mrs. Ebersole. He should never have underestimated Mrs. Black. He'd thought the threat to her reputation might be enough, but it seemed she was made of much sterner stuff.

And possessed such a lovely mouth. Especially today. When she smiled.

It was almost worth stepping in rooster dung.

Almost.

Chapter Seven

"Mrs. Ebersole. A word, if you please." Drew addressed the bulldog of a housekeeper, who regarded him as if he were some sort of vermin invading the house. If he wasn't careful, she'd chase him with a broom.

"Mr. Sinclair." Mrs. Ebersole bobbed politely. "What can I get for you?"

Drew's suffering had stretched out an entire week. King George crowing just beneath his window before the sun even rose. Copious amounts of chicken dung, among other types of animal refuse, seemed to appear no matter what route he took to walk the fields or view the barns and other outbuildings. Cabbage served at every meal. Yesterday, the offending vegetable had been snuck inside the scrambled eggs he'd requested for breakfast.

Drew regarded the housekeeper of Blackbird Heath. She was a slightly sour, mannish looking woman who often smelled of tobacco or onions. He imagined her walking about outside in the evenings, smoking a cheroot and managing to avoid the chicken dung. Her opinion of Drew was akin to Mrs. Black's.

"I was wondering, Mrs. Ebersole, if we could discuss the dinner menu."

"The dinner menu?"

"I would like future meals to be absent of cabbage, if you please."

"But—" her bushy brows drew together in confusion. "You insisted I serve it at every meal. It's one of your favorites."

Drew cocked his head. "When did I ask you to do so?" Had he had too much wine one night while pouring through the ledgers in the study? No, not even completely foxed would Drew ask for cabbage.

"Well, *you* didn't sir. Not directly. You requested it of Mrs. Black, and she in turn, informed me of your preferences. Cabbage at every meal."

That little—"Didn't you notice, Mrs. Ebersole, that I never eat any of it? In fact, I won't even allow one leaf to touch my plate?"

Mrs. Ebersole raised a brow. "I did wonder considering Mrs. Black claimed it to be your favorite. But I thought maybe I wasn't preparing it as you're accustomed to."

"I'm accustomed to not eating it. Ever." Drew ran a hand through his hair. "I know Blackbird Heath is famed for its cabbage, but I beg you, no more."

"Wasn't always," Mrs. Ebersole offered. "Famed for cabbage."

Drew knew that from Patchahoo's research, but there seemed to be some discrepancy as to when Blackbird Heath had become more working farm than a lord's country retreat. "This was once the estate of a baron, was it not?"

"Lord Marker. But that was before the Roundheads."

"Oh, yes. Dreadful fellows."

Mrs. Ebersole shot him a look. "Lord Marker lost his estate and his head. The Blacks were staunch supporters of Cromwell and awarded this land. They renamed the property Blackbird Heath. The family fortunes took a hit once Cromwell was gone and something else had to be done. Built the barns and mill. Planted crops and kept sheep to keep them whole. Mr. Black, God rest his soul, never cared much for his home, which is why I imagine he wagered it." She dared him to say differently. "And why you're determined to sell it. I wish you all the luck with that, Mr. Sinclair."

The housekeeper gave him a militant look before tromping off.

Damn.

Just when Drew thought he and Mrs. Ebersole were getting on. Endless plates of cabbage were in his future.

<hr />

"Mr. Godwick, how lovely to see you." Hester greeted Martin Godwick with little enthusiasm. It really wasn't Martin's fault that he called at a bad time. Hester had only just finished up a difficult birth with one of her prize cows and had been looking forward to simply resting for an hour after a hasty bath. Martin arrived just as she finished making herself presentable once more.

Martin had taken over Godwick & Sons, his father having been Joshua's solicitor. Godwick senior had died mere months after Joshua, so Martin had assumed the role and become Hester's solicitor. Martin was convinced that Joshua's will should not have been altered due to his declining mental state and blamed Godwick senior for allowing it. Given enough time, Martin thought he could find a judge who might be amenable to hearing Hester's case, but thus far he had been unsuccessful. She appreciated that Martin continued to press the matter, because Hester had no one else to turn to. He'd been a good friend, her only friend, even before Joshua's death.

Martin's wife Ellie was another matter.

"A poor greeting." He took her hand. "Considering I've brought you something." Martin held out a small tin of sweets. "Ellie brought them back with her from Grantham, lest you think I've done something kind."

"How thoughtful of Ellie." And unusual. She usually regarded Hester as a cross she must bear. "She must be feeling better if she ventured to Grantham to visit her parents."

Martin's face instantly clouded.

"Ellie is better, isn't she?" Hester inquired.

"Ellie's mother took her to a physician of some renown in Grantham. One of the best. We had such high hopes. But Dr. Burger can find no reason for her stomach pains. I'm at wit's end. Ellie came home from Grantham quite distressed. She had a cup of tea and then immediately retired to her room."

"I'm so sorry, Martin."

The mysterious illness of his wife had affected Martin greatly. A stomach ailment that would improve for a few days, only to send Ellie to bed once more after a light meal. The illness had confounded her doctors in Horncastle. "Is there anything I can do?"

"I expect I'll need to take Ellie to London if she doesn't improve soon." He gave her a weak smile. "I try to keep her as comfortable as possible."

Hester took a seat, motioning for Martin to do the same. "I'll assume you are here about Mr. Sinclair."

"There's a rumor…" Martin's light blue eyes trailed over her with concern. "That Mr. Sinclair is living here. Under the same roof as you. I've reminded anyone who asks that you were devoted to Mr. Black and would hardly entertain such an improper living arrangement."

"I know there are some in Horncastle who still see me as the daughter of Thomas Morton, a philandering sot but—in this case, I'm afraid the gossips are correct." Hester bit her lip. "Sinclair has taken up residence, though it is only a ploy to force me to leave Blackbird Heath."

"Unacceptable." Martin stood with a furious jerking motion. "Completely indecent. You must leave, Hester. You can stay with me and Ellie."

"You know what will happen if I vacate Blackbird Heath of my own accord. Sinclair can then sell the farm and I can't allow it." Hester didn't bother to mention that it was unlikely Ellie would be thrilled to have her as a guest. "We rarely interact with each other. I'm making his existence here as uncomfortable as possible. He'll eventually become bored and return to London. Sinclair is too much of a dandy to wish to stay here longer."

Martin sat once more and took her hand. "There must be something I can do. Tell me, Hester, and I will do it."

He was so earnest. So determined to help her. What would she do without Martin?

"Find a judge who will listen. There must be a way to declare the will Joshua dictated shortly before his death invalid."

Martin's chin lifted, his attention fixed on something outside the parlor window. "Is that him? Sinclair?"

Hester turned to see a cart pulling up before the front door bearing two trunks as Sinclair strode around the corner to greet the driver. He really had sent to London for his things. She'd been secretly hoping he'd changed his mind.

"Yes. I'm afraid it is."

Sinclair placed several coins in the driver's hand, smiling the entire time. Instead of calling for Dobbins or Jake, Sinclair first discarded his coat, tossing it over a bush next to the front door. Then he picked up one of the trunks, the muscles rippling beneath the fabric of the shirt as he hefted the trunk over one shoulder. A charming smile pulled at his lips as he said something amusing to the cart driver. The strands of his dark hair gleamed in the afternoon sun, thick and wavy, curling about his ears. She could make out the mossy green of his eyes even through the window.

Dewy warmth curled inside Hester, pulsing with unexpected longing. She looked down at her lap, struck by the reaction to the mere sight of Sinclair in his shirtsleeves. Wholly ridiculous. Hester managed a working farm. Animals copulated. Many of the laborers she hired went about in their shirtsleeves. She'd even seen a couple without shirts, tossing buckets of water over each other when the weather grew terribly warm. The point being, Sinclair in his shirtsleeves was nothing Hester hadn't seen before.

Another soft ache fluttered low in her belly.

"He appears to be making himself at home," Martin said in a frigid tone. "It isn't right."

"Sinclair owns Blackbird Heath. Unfortunately, he has as much right to live here as I do. I'm not sure what Joshua could have been thinking." Hester shook her head, lips pursing. "Giving some stranger my home, but with another swoop of the pen declaring I didn't have to leave unless I wished it. Perhaps he sought to punish me."

"Joshua Black wasn't of sound mind." Martin turned back to her. "He couldn't have been to make such a decision. That is the case I have been making. But because my father actually drafted the revised will, it makes overturning it that much more difficult. He was highly regarded and known for being above doing anything remotely unscrupulous. Had it been any other solicitor I would have no issue with questioning their motives. Maybe I could put out that my father's health was failing or—"

"No." Hester interrupted with a touch to his arm. "You cannot damage Godwick & Sons or your own reputation, Martin. Especially not for my sake." Her eyes lifted to the sight of Sinclair and the cart driver hauling in the larger trunk from the cart. "Eventually, he will return to London. He hates the country. And cabbage." She smiled. "I've instructed Mrs. Ebersole to make sure to have cabbage served at every meal."

Martin laughed, though the amusement didn't reach his eyes, which were still on Sinclair.

"Well, if cabbage doesn't work, Hester, I'll think of something else."

CHAPTER EIGHT

ANOTHER WEEK SLIPPED by, with Hester increasingly annoyed that Sinclair seemed in no hurry to vacate Blackbird Heath. He roamed about the farm, engaging in conversation with everyone save Hester, and when not observing the sheep or the potatoes growing, Sinclair disappeared into the study. At first, she'd worried about him reviewing the ledgers but Joshua had only ever expressed a passing interest in them. Men like her husband and Sinclair rarely worried over where their coin came from, only that they received it.

Also irritating, Hester's ploy with the cabbage had failed. Mrs. Ebersole had reluctantly admitted Mr. Sinclair had confronted her on the matter. Cabbage was still served, but not in excess amounts. King George seemed to have little effect on Sinclair's sleep. In fact, Hester had deliberately removed the rooster back to his usual spot so that he wouldn't awaken the entire household.

Which meant Sinclair would also likely still be asleep.

Perfect for her plans.

Silently, Hester made her way up the stairs, each step filled with determination. Tucking the small, wiggling sack more firmly against her side, Hester quietly made her way down the hall to Sinclair's room. The idea had come to her two days ago while walking to check on the pigs and hearing the beasts squeal in terror.

A smile tugged at her lips.

Piles of dung placed nearly everywhere that Sinclair might walk hadn't worked. Nor cabbage or the extreme boredom of the countryside, but possibly, her latest gambit *might*. If she were lucky, after she placed the sack in his room, Mr. Sinclair would decline to spend another night at Blackbird Heath.

"Stop that," Hester whispered to the twisting sack as she tiptoed to Sinclair's room. "We have an agreement. You frighten him half out of his wits and slink off somewhere. Pretend to be fierce."

Dawn was just starting to pink the sky. The house dark and still. Hester turned the knob to Sinclair's door, gratified to hear not a squeak of the hinges. She'd had the foresight to oil the hinges yesterday while Sinclair walked along the sugar beet fields pretending interest in her crops. Opening the door to Sinclair's room, Hester stepped inside.

The scent of cedar and leather filled her nostrils as she carefully stepped over his boots. Sinclair was sleeping on his stomach, his arms stretched out on either side, sprawled across the bed. The sheets were twisted about his hips.

Her heart thumped hard inside her chest.

The broad line of Sinclair's back lay exposed, a collection of sculpted hollows of muscle and curved sinew. The shock of thick hair, the same color as fresh gingerbread covered his eyes and cascaded over his cheeks. Long, elegant fingers were stretched out in Hester's direction.

Her fist tightened on the sack she carried.

Goodness, he was beautiful.

He is the enemy. Best to remember that no matter how splendid he looked shirtless.

She crept towards the bed and lifted just the edge of the sheet. Opening the sack, Hester released the grass snake before she could lose her nerve. The sheets moved as the snake, thrilled to be free, started to explore.

Perfect. Now Hester only had to get out of Sinclair's room and down the stairs before her little friend made his presence known. She backed away, so intent on watching the tiny snake move beneath the sheets, Hester didn't remember the boots she'd stepped over moments ago were right behind her. She tripped, her backside hitting the floor with a thud, and cursed. Rather loudly.

Thomas Morton wasn't much of a father, but he had taught Hester how to curse.

That's probably what woke up Sinclair. The cursing. Not the snake.

One of Sinclair's eyes, like the leaves in the depths of the forest, peered through the tangle of his hair. His fingers curled on the bed sheet. He twisted gracefully, muscles rippling as he moved, never once looking away from Hester and reached into the sheets. Sitting up in one fluid move, Sinclair held up the poor, wiggling grass snake.

"Good morning, Mrs. Black." The words held a hint of amusement, but nothing remotely friendly shone in his handsome features.

"Good morning," she whispered, horrified to the very depths of her being at being caught.

"I'll assume this belongs to you." He held the grass snake up higher, mossy gaze flicking to the sack clutched in her hands.

Hester lifted her chin. She could brave this out. Possibly. There wasn't any good excuse why she would be in his room with a snake except the obvious. "Indeed. I was attempting to retrieve him."

"Were you?" The side of his mouth twitched. "Retrieving him?"

She nodded. "I—use him to patrol the kitchen garden."

"The kitchen garden. Which is outside this house and not my room." A lopsided smile pulled at his lips. Oh, yes. He was amused. But not in a good way.

Hester's pulse fluttered softly within the confines of her chest. She found Sinclair annoyingly attractive, but seeing him bare-chested, with a dusting of dark hair spread across his torso, barely awake and rumpled, did something quite unexpected to her insides.

Still holding the snake, Sinclair gracefully slid out of the bed, the sheets dipping away from his hips.

Oh dear.

Sinclair was naked beneath the sheets. Completely.

Gaze still fixed on her, Sinclair came forward, seemingly oblivious to the fact he was naked before her.

No, he knows. He just doesn't care.

Masculine beauty wasn't something Hester often contemplated. It wasn't that she didn't appreciate the male form, but rather a great many other things took precedence. There was little time to think of physical relations with the opposite sex when you were far too busy making sure the cabbages were free of aphids or the bees were producing enough honey. The harsh indentation of Sinclair's hipbones stood out, accentuating his lean form. A dusting of dark hair along his chest narrowed and fell below his navel to—

Hester looked up at the ceiling. She managed a working farm. She had been married. She knew what the male appendage looked like. But *good lord.*

A soft chuckle sounded. "Is there something above the bed that interests you?"

"Water stain. I must have a leak in the roof." She cleared her throat. "If you please cover yourself, sir. This is inappropriate at best."

"I believe this is my room, Mrs. Black," he interrupted her. "If your senses are offended, that is entirely your own fault. As a land manager," he said in a mocking tone. "You gave me the impression you were familiar with all aspects of animal husbandry."

"I am." She lowered her gaze but kept it fixed on his face. Hester was rarely embarrassed by displays of mating. But those were horses. Cows. Pigs, even. Not—

"Hand me the sack so that you can take your friend back to the gardens where he belongs."

Hester's arm shot out, but she tilted her chin, refusing to look at him further. The warmth of his fingers brushed hers as he dropped the snake inside.

"I have two brothers, Mrs. Black. One older, the other is my twin."

She cleared her throat at the thought of two such spectacular men parading about. "A twin brother?"

"Oh, don't worry, he doesn't look a thing like me, but that is hardly the point. Snakes in one's bed among brothers is a common prank. Frogs work well too, if you're interested. The occasional lizard. I grew up in the country. I thought I mentioned that fact to you."

He hadn't. Or if he did, Hester failed to note it. Sinclair seemed like such a card playing dandy, a man accustomed to life in town, so completely out of place in Lincolnshire that she hadn't considered he'd not been born in London.

"If you really wanted to get rid of me, you should have used an adder, not some poor grass snake. Let me guess. I was to pop from my bed, screaming and flapping about. Terrified, as if I was a proper young lady with a spider in her hair. You would then, sadly, inform me that the house is infested with snakes. Or there was a nest in my room. I'd be forced to seek other accommodations or give up completely because Blackbird Heath is a frightening place. I'm rather insulted you think me such a milksop."

"I wasn't trying to—"

"Catch me unclothed?" A rolling bit of laughter came out of him, floating like warm water over Hester's skin. "Good lord, look at the blush on your cheeks. You, who run a bloody farm."

"Yes, but there is a great deal of difference between a stallion and you, Mr. Sinclair."

He shrugged. "Not in my estimation."

What an arrogant—"I am not," Hester annunciated every word before turning to look directly at him. She assessed him slowly, lips tight, tamping down the flowering arousal between her thighs. He was goading her, and Hester would not allow it. "The *least* prudish. As you have so kindly reminded me, I manage a farm. I am a widow. And I am not at all impressed with your vulgar display."

Sinclair loomed over her, so male. Big. Somewhat intimidating. Things appeared far larger than she would have anticipated.

Arousal brushed over her skin once more.

"My face is up here, Mrs. Black."

Hester inhaled slowly, instructing her lungs to fill with air. The attraction for Sinclair bloomed in the small confines of the bedroom no matter how much she didn't wish it.

He inhaled sharply as something heated flashed in his eyes, mirroring her own desire.

She took a very deliberate step backward, taking the sack with her.

The blood beneath her skin pulsed as honey spread along her limbs. This sensation, strong enough to make her legs weak, was an alien feeling. One she'd never felt for a man. Certainly, not her husband.

"Don't nibble on your lip in such a way, Mrs. Black." The sleep roughened command caught her off guard. "Because it tempts me to do so." There was no mockery in the words, only a blatant declaration of intent.

Hester shut her eyes. She wanted to thread her fingers through the hair decorating his torso and trace the line of his hipbones. "Please return to your bed," she said, without opening her eyes. "Cover yourself. It is improper to prance about in such a way."

The scent of him crept into her nostrils as he moved towards her. Warm male mixed with cedar and soap.

"And would you join me, Mrs. Black?"

The words curled around Hester, inviting a host of temptations. Visions of two naked bodies, twisted in ecstasy on the bed flashed before her. Sinclair's talents were not limited to cards, she surmised, instructing her body to stop pulsing in his direction.

"No, thank you," she replied crisply. "Please cover yourself."

The sound of his bare feet padding back to the bed sounded, along with the sheets moving.

"You can open your eyes now, Mrs. Black. I'm quite decent."

Hester peered at him, lounging against the headboard. Sinclair had pulled the bedcovers up to his chin, leaving one foot sticking out, toes wiggling mischievously in her direction.

Sinclair thumped the mattress. "Lumpy thing, but I fixed it. Someone had stuck several large rocks beneath the stuffing. I can't imagine who."

"Neither can I," she replied. Mrs. Ebersole was the most likely culprit. The housekeeper was as eager to get rid of Sinclair as Hester.

He cocked his head, deep brown curls the color of warm gingerbread just out of the oven toppling over his brow. "I suggest you take your friend outside, Mrs. Black." Sinclair rolled over, giving her his back, and settled back into his pillow. "Unless you've changed your mind about joining me?"

Hester sniffed in disdain. "You are a flagrant rake in addition to being a charlatan." No decent gentleman would stand naked before her without so much as blinking. Or invite her into his bed.

"Oh, I'm much worse than that, Mrs. Black. I'm a sin."

She wasn't sure how to respond to such an odd comment, so Hester merely turned and strode out of the room, not bothering to be quiet.

Sinclair wasn't a sin, but the very devil himself.

Chapter Nine

Drew rode into the town of Horncastle after having considered little else during the entire trip but Mrs. Hester Black. The attraction to her, apparent at their first meeting, hadn't shifted in the least, but only intensified, even after her childish attempts to get him to leave Blackbird Heath. The snake was particularly inspired. Sneaking about his room while he was asleep, intent on wreaking havoc, Hester had gotten a bit more than she'd expected.

So had Drew.

The sight of her, blushing and stammering, copper tendrils floating over her annoyed cheeks, was the most arousing thing he'd witnessed in some time. He hadn't quite decided *why* Hester had such a pronounced effect on him. Outside of the red hair, there was nothing physically appealing about her. Drew, as a rule, preferred his women rounded. Generously endowed. Soft. If there was anything soft about Hester, Drew had yet to find it.

Under her skirts, perhaps. Or the underside of one breast.

A bolt of pure lust shot down between his thighs. He wanted to wrestle Hester to the bed. Or the floor. Bed her in some grassy field. There had to be one free of animal dung somewhere.

Drew's lips curled in disgust. What on earth was wrong with him?

Hester was the only woman he'd seen, outside of Mrs. Ebersole and a mousy little maid named Mary, since coming to Blackbird Heath His attraction was nothing more than a lack of female companionship,

Drew told himself. A good ale or better, actual Irish whiskey, if he could find it in this remote place, would set him to rights. Or a lovely widow.

Not Mrs. Hester Black. Who was not lovely. At all.

Today's meeting wouldn't take a great deal of time. Mr. Scoggins, a local landowner, had long coveted Blackbird Heath and he had the proper resources to make the estate profitable. Patchahoo had identified him as the person most likely to purchase the property. Scoggins had the funds to modernize Blackbird Heath and the financial prowess to make the farm much more profitable. Hester might know crops and bees, but her keeping of the ledgers left much to be desired. Drew had found multiple errors in the ledgers and couldn't tell if the mistakes were made purposefully or not.

What mattered was what sort of offer Scoggins might make.

Drew patted the letters in his pocket. There was one for his brother Jordan explaining that business would keep him in Lincolnshire for the time being. The other, was to his friends in London. Hester deserved to have a taste of her own medicine.

And he wasn't going to use a snake.

>>><<<

IT WAS ALREADY mid-afternoon when Drew finished with Scoggins. The meeting with the boisterous gentleman had taken far longer than he'd anticipated. Scoggins was a friendly sort, and their discussion flowed nearly as well as the ale and food at the Maid's Inn. The excellent roast lamb had been accompanied by carrots and potatoes, along with stewed apples. Not so much as a leaf of cabbage in sight. Scoggins had been a fount of information about Blackbird Heath and Hester Black.

The Widow Black did not have many friends in Horncastle.

Hester Morton had been the only child of a card playing sot with a philandering reputation prior to her marriage to Joshua Black. She'd been raised on a farm just outside of Horncastle that had belonged to her grandfather. Thomas Morton, Hester's father, knew little about farming. Less about cards or dice. He spent most of his time at a local tavern and not working his land. By the time Hester's mother died, Morton had stripped his father's farm of nearly everything that was worth selling. Morton and his red-haired daughter were a familiar sight in Horncastle as he dragged Hester from one hovel to the next as his fortunes declined. Dressed in rags and left to beg for coin, she became a subject of pity and scorn.

Joshua Black had been a confirmed bachelor before his marriage to Hester, which had come as a surprise. Some said Thomas Morton offered Hester as payment for a debt he owed Black but most of Horncastle derided her as nothing more than an ambitious young woman seeking an escape from poverty. The marriage brought her some respectability but not much.

Black was rarely in residence, leaving his young wife to run the farm which he bled to maintain his indulgent lifestyle. It was no great secret in Horncastle. Hester rarely came into town except to visit her solicitor, Martin Godwick. She had no friends to speak of. No family. Not one person or family in Horncastle had ever attempted to help her, judging Hester for her parentage and not for herself.

Drew had listened to the entire tale without flinching. Scoggins spoke of Hester with more than a little disdain, his scorn for her and the impoverished child she'd been evident in every word. An unexpected surge of protectiveness filled him for Hester. Drew knew well what it was to be looked down on. Gossiped about. Treated as if you were something less because of who your parents were. The Sinclairs hadn't had to resort to begging, but only because Jordan started raising pigs and fighting with his fists to win a purse when he needed. Tamsin raced her horse. Malcolm became a soldier so he could send money back to them all. Drew gambled. Aurora, bless her, tended the much unloved cabbage patch at Dunnings.

He left Scoggins at the Maid's Inn, promising that the landowner would be the first to know when Blackbird Heath was for sale.

If I sell it.

Drew pushed the thought away. Of course he still meant to sell the farm.

While the afternoon had helped shift his opinion of Hester and gave him a deeper appreciation for her love of Blackbird Heath, it didn't change his mind. There was no need to keep a farm he didn't want or the redhead that came with it, not when Worth and the partnership he offered was Drew's future.

But she blushed so prettily.

Honestly, his annoyance that Hester had stooped to put a snake in his bed had been so sharp that the last thing he'd considered was his nakedness. But the longer he stood before her, watching the soft rose creep across her cheeks to color her skin, Drew felt the pull of attraction to her.

I want to tup her.

"Damn."

Drew had flirted with the buxom lass serving he and Scoggins earlier. She was nicely rounded, smiled and made no effort to hide her interest in him, yet he'd felt nothing.

Bloody hell.

His theory that he only desired Hester because no other females save Mrs. Ebersole were in the immediate vicinity wasn't true at all. Drew had wanted to bed Hester Black barely ten minutes after making her acquaintance. She'd survived much worse than Dunnings. A drunkard for a father. Poverty. The sheer determination to keep Black from selling the estate so he could indulge his love of cards alone was a sign of her resilience.

No wonder Hester was so bloody hostile. In her mind, Drew was yet another gambling wastrel determined to take Blackbird Heath. Her home. Likely the only one she'd ever had.

Drew strode down the street and turned the corner into a short alley, ignoring the twinge of guilt over Hester. He'd left his horse near the smithy when he posted his letters, choosing to make the short walk to the Maid's Inn. As he entered the alley, a stone rolled back into the back of Drew's booted foot. A push followed, directly in the center of his back as someone tried to force him to the ground.

He stumbled, but quickly regained his footing. Drew lived in London and was often out late at night and was no stranger to thieves and footpads wanting his purse. He only hadn't expected to be attacked in Horncastle.

The hair along his cheek lifted as the slice of a blade narrowly missed his neck. Drew instinctively dropped to the ground and rolled. Kicking out his leg, the toe of his boot made contact with his assailant's knee. Rolling to his back, he kicked out with his heel as the thief's knee gave way and caught the man in the chin. Drew came to his feet and delivered a sharp kick to the man's stomach.

The thug made an attempt to slash out with the knife again, aiming for Drew's thigh.

He ground his heel into the man's wrist. "Drop the knife."

The man on the ground grunted, wiggling about and trying to dislodge Drew's hold on his wrist. He wore a mask, one that covered most of his features outside of his eyes.

"If you don't release the knife, I'll break your wrist. It won't be pleasant."

The thug shook his head and continued to struggle. He grabbed at Drew's ankle trying to push him away.

"Very well." The heel of Drew's boot ground into the thug's wrist. "I did warn you." A satisfying snap filled the alley along with the man's scream of pain.

As Drew had told Hester, he'd grown up with two brothers, both heavier and broader through the chest and he'd learned to defend himself from a young age. The three Sinclair boys were known for brawling both at River Crest and in London well before their father's death and the banishment to Dunnings. There was a reason the Sinclairs were nicknamed The Deadly Sins and had a reputation for being uncivilized. Drew recalled quite clearly pummeling a snotty lad in the park one day after the overprivileged twit had the *audacity* to sneer that Lady Emerson, Drew's mother, was a *whore*.

Yes, Drew liked good food. Well-tailored clothing. Expensive boots. Cleanliness in general. But he was the furthest thing from a dandy.

"You could have simply dropped the knife." Drew reached down and plucked the blade from the man's fingers. This wasn't the first time someone had attempted to take his purse by force, nor did he think it the last. He slid the knife into his pocket and stepped back.

"Go on, then. Leave before I display my own skills with a blade."

Whimpering sounded at his feet.

Drew sighed and leaned back against the wall. Reaching inside his coat, he drew forth a cheroot. He lit the tip with a flick of his wrist, sending the used match in the direction of his assailant.

The man got to his feet, glaring at Drew his injured wrist clutched to his chest. "You'll be sorry about this," he sneered before jogging away.

"I don't think I will." He blew out a puff of smoke, finding it odd that there had been no demand for money or valuables during the entire skirmish. A novice at thievery to be sure. Wouldn't survive a day in London.

Taking a draw of the cheroot, he shrugged and strolled out onto the main street to collect his horse.

Chapter Ten

Hester yawned once more and half-stumbled her way down the stairs. She'd overslept, a rare occurrence and one that left her groggy and out of sorts. The entire night had been spent tossing and turning, the image of Sinclair's nakedness invading what should have been a peaceful evening. In an effort to avoid him and further speculate about what he looked like without clothing, she'd eaten in the kitchen and taken a glass of brandy back to her room. Which didn't do the least bit of good.

A *gentleman* would have wrapped the sheets about him. Or begged her to turn. Not strutted naked towards her with a snake grasped in one outstretched hand.

Hester's nails dug into the wood of the banister as she steadied herself.

The entire incident was made worse by the fact that Hester *had* invaded Sinclair's bedroom. If anyone were to find out, there wasn't an explanation she could give to justify her actions. Not even Mrs. Ebersole would understand. Martin would be absolutely horrified.

When re-examined in the cold light of day, after a sleepless night, Hester had to agree that placing a snake in a gentleman's bed with the sole purpose of terrifying him into leaving Blackbird Heath was ridiculous and childish.

More importantly, it hadn't worked.

There had to be some way to induce Sinclair to leave and continue to allow her to run Blackbird Heath. They could not coexist together forever.

A warm tingle shot down her spine at the thought of him two rooms down, for months on end.

"There you are, Mrs. Black." Sinclair's voice floated to the doorway of the dining room where he was eating breakfast. "You overslept. I grew worried that you were ill."

His overly polite tone combined with his usual magnificent appearance irritated Hester to no end. Never a hair out of place. Cravat, perfect. If she leaned down, Hester would likely see her reflection in the shine of his boots.

"Mr. Sinclair." Hester greeted him, bumping into the table at the thought of what lie beneath all that fine clothing.

"Do I have something on my cheek?" he said in that silky tone, brushing the line of his jaw.

"No," she snapped.

"You're staring." He wiggled his brows just a bit.

"I'm only surprised to find you up so early." Taking a seat, she reached for a piece of toast.

"Come now, Mrs. Black. Let's not make things awkward concerning your visit to my room yesterday. You are a widow, after all. And a farmer. I doubt there's anything you haven't seen before."

A wash of heat crept up her chest and neck. "Not at all."

"Wonderful. I hope you don't have plans for Mrs. Ebersole today. I've need of her," he said with just a hint of innuendo before giving her housekeeper a flirtatious wink.

Mrs. Ebersole bared her teeth and grunted.

"What would you need Mrs. Ebersole for?" Hester's lips pulled together.

"Preparations."

"Preparations?" This was bound to be unpleasant.

"Goodness, you sound like a parrot." He took a forkful of eggs.

"I'm having a little house party here at Blackbird Heath. Well, more an excuse to play cards while watching the chickens, I suppose. You were correct in assuming I'd grow bored in the country, so I've invited some of my friends from London for a visit."

Shocked, Hester couldn't think of how to respond. London gentlemen invading the sanctity of her home? To play cards? In Lincolnshire? Good lord, what if Sinclair wagered Blackbird Heath?

"Would you mind passing over the currant jelly?" he drawled.

Her fingers closed over the jar, considering what would happen if she bludgeoned him with it while he enjoyed his eggs. Mrs. Ebersole would clean up the mess. Probably help Hester hide the body.

She pushed the jelly across the table.

"Thank you." The green of his eyes landed on her, warmth and amusement dancing in the depths.

The delicious feeling, like spooling honey sank into her skin, sliding down between her breasts to tighten into a loose knot between her thighs. Insistently fluttering no matter how she pushed her legs together.

"I hardly think Blackbird Heath an appropriate destination for a house party, Sinclair. What will you do, throw dice while I milk the cows in the barn?" Hester had terrible visions of finely dressed idiots tramping through her fields. Scaring her chickens. Making Mrs. Ebersole wish to commit murder.

Sinclair put down his fork. "Blackbird Heath is lovely for all that you've turned this once stately manor into a farm."

"I didn't—" Hester tried to put a damper on her rising anger. "If you think that inviting a troupe of gin-swilling card players to prance around in the manure for a few days will induce me to vacate the premises, you are incorrect." She tossed down her toast.

"I hadn't imagined you to be so dramatic. Gin swilling? Brandy, perhaps. French wine, at the very least. I'm having trouble locating the whiskey I happen to enjoy. Mrs. Ebersole will come up with an adequate menu. But no cabbage." His eyes narrowed on her.

This was ridiculous. Blackbird Heath was a farm. Not a sanctuary for card players from London. "How do you expect to pay for this house party?"

"How do you think, Mrs. Black?" Sinclair picked up his fork once more. "As you've so often told me, the estate is profitable. My friends and I may find being in the country so amusing Blackbird Heath might become a regular destination. I could hold a house party at least twice a year, possibly more."

Hester's mouth popped open.

"I've finally made you speechless with excitement." The corner of his mouth lifted in a mischievous grin. "Thankfully, I've found an excellent purveyor of spirits in Horncastle. Don't worry, I won't overtax Mrs. Ebersole. Depending on how things go." Sinclair took another bite of eggs. "I'll hire a chef and extra servants."

The expense for nothing more than amusement. "The farm can't afford—"

"I disagree." A commanding note entered the previously jovial conversation and his eyes took on the hardness of emeralds. "After all, I've examined the ledgers."

A squeak came from Hester.

"This is the arrangement you wished, isn't it? I take the majority of the profits for my pursuits, and you manage *my* property."

Yes, but she hadn't expected him to actually look at the ledgers to see how much was at his disposal. Joshua rarely did. After a time, he simply took whatever she offered. But if she'd known Sinclair would actually review the accounts, she would have made *adjustments*. As she had with her husband.

"I can see that your previous offer no longer seems so agreeable. Two of my guests are financiers in London. It is their opinion I should sell Blackbird Heath, but perhaps you can convince them why I should not."

Hester tossed down her toast. The alternative, Hester supposed, would be to tolerate a round of snooty Londoners invading her home, disturbing her animals and crops. The bees didn't do well when interrupted in their honey making. Mrs. Ebersole was an adequate housekeeper but unprepared to prepare the sort of lavish meals Sinclair would demand. Hester wasn't even sure they had enough linens for all the beds. The other rooms upstairs had been shut up for years.

"I'm not leaving, Mr. Sinclair," she finally bit out.

"I don't expect you will," he answered, once more digging into his eggs.

Chapter Eleven

Drew struggled not to laugh and spit out his mouthful of eggs. Hester was woefully transparent. She'd be a terrible card player. The upcoming invasion had so thoroughly unsettled her that her luscious mouth had pulled into a tiny, tight rosette. Not to mention the way she kept eyeing the jar of currant jelly as if it were a weapon.

Honestly, the thought of Hester attacking him over the breakfast table was highly arousing. Those sleek legs, usually only discerned through a pair of baggy men's trousers she sometimes wore, would wrap tightly, strangling him like that poor garden snake had attempted to. They'd both be naked, of course. She'd be intent on murdering him and—

"Have you ever been to the Maid's Inn, Mrs. Black?" Drew said nonchalantly, regarding her from beneath his lashes. It was an unwelcome thought that Hester despised him so much she'd send a hired thug after him.

"The Maid's Inn?" Her cheeks pinked. "Is that in Horncastle?"

Drew watched her, trying to discern any hint of guilt. She was blushing but—"Yes, in Horncastle."

She shrugged not looking him in the eye. "I haven't been to Horncastle in some time. Blackbird Heath keeps me quite busy. Even if I did venture to town, I doubt I'd have reason to visit an inn."

"They have excellent lamb. I thought perhaps you'd sampled their fare. Quite good." Drew immediately regretted the words, belatedly recalling that Hester had once begged for scraps at the back door of the Maid's Inn. "I only meant—"

Hester colored further. "I'm afraid I have not dined there," her voice was small. Pained. She lifted her chin to Drew. "Perhaps you should share your findings with Mrs. Ebersole," Hester replied, trying not to smile. "I'm sure she'd welcome your suggestions."

Mrs. Ebersole would be more likely to roast Drew on a spit much like the lamb. And he would deserve it for saying such a thing to Hester, meant or not.

"Perhaps I will. Don't let me keep you from your chores." Drew went back to his eggs. "I'm sure King George and his harem need feeding. Potatoes need to be protected from blight."

Hester had picked up her tea, but the cup paused mere inches from her lips, blinking at him. "Blight?" Her brows drew together.

Drew had been walking the fields first out of curiosity and then out of genuine interest. When at Dunnings, his family had tried a list of crops, but anything save cabbage refused to grow in profusion. The small plot of potatoes Aurora attempted to grow thrived until signs of blight appeared. She'd cried for days over those damned potatoes.

"I grew up in the country. I know I've mentioned it to you."

"Yes, but—"

"I know quite a bit more than the average *wastrel*, Mrs. Black." Drew's experience with blight had been brief, but he knew a great deal about the worms that liked to feast on cabbage. A farmer near Dunnings had offered his help when the cabbage became infested. There was nothing that could be done for the potatoes.

"Northumberland. That would be my guess."

Drew's fingers tightened on his fork.

"The posh London accent you affect slips at times." She gave him a knowing look, waiting for him to respond.

He tried so hard to hide Dunnings from everyone, but of course, this little harridan had figured it out. Well, that was fine. He knew a great deal about Hester now as well thanks to Scoggins. They had more in common than she could possibly imagine.

"A good guess, Northumberland." Drew didn't bother to elaborate further. He didn't care to discuss Dunnings or Spittal. Just the thought had spoiled his breakfast.

The silence between them lengthened until Hester fidgeted in her chair before finally coming to her feet. "If you'll excuse me, I need to see to my crops."

He knew from viewing the potato field and speaking to Dobbins, one of the farmhands, that Hester resolutely refused to give up on the potatoes though the blight was becoming apparent. She seemed to think digging up the infected plants would save them all, but it wouldn't. He should allow her the folly. It was as blatantly foolish as her proposal to be his land manager. "Burn the smaller field, Mrs. Black," he said quietly. "If you do not, you will lose all."

"What do you care, Mr. Sinclair?" she returned stiffly. "If all my potatoes go bad, if my sugar beets rot, if my hens stop laying, what do you care?"

"I don't want the value of the estate to be affected," he retorted, setting his fork down with a clang.

Hester spun on her heel and left the dining room. The back door slammed shut a few moments later.

Drew sat back, pushing away the plate of eggs. Even if Dunnings hadn't spoiled his appetite, Mrs. Ebersole had used too much pepper. A show of her dislike.

Hester marched past the window, skirts flapping about her legs. The sun glinted on her hair, turning some of the strands aflame and lighting her strong, determined features. She was headed towards the fields but would probably stop to check on the hens and King George first. She wouldn't take the advice to burn the field because Drew had given it.

"I am, after all, nothing more than a card playing wastrel," he mused out loud.

"You said it, Mr. Sinclair. Not I." Mrs. Ebersole appeared at his shoulder. "The wastrel bit." A deep sigh came from the housekeeper. "But I agree with you, the field should be burned. The blight will spread to the other fields. I've told her so myself. I suppose you won't be wanting any cabbage served for your highbrow friends, will you?"

Drew considered the older woman. What would she do if he sold Blackbird Heath? Or Dobbins? Jake? The little maid who rushed out of his way whenever she caught sight of him? "Mrs. Ebersole, where would you go if I sold the farm?"

The housekeeper's eyes grew pained, her features tightening, reminding Drew of a troll. She was a remarkably unattractive woman. But her eyes blazed with the same defiance that lit Hester's. "Won't be your concern, will it, Mr. Sinclair?"

"I suppose not."

The problem with selling Blackbird Heath, Drew was coming to realize, wasn't *exclusively* Hester Black. Mrs. Ebersole didn't like him, but that didn't mean he was in a hurry to throw her out.

"May I have some coffee, please? And no cabbage for my friends."

Guilt, once a mere tiny seed, started to sprout inside him. He would need to make provisions for Hester and her employees when he sold Blackbird Heath, else he was no better than Bentley.

That was if he could ever get Hester to leave Blackbird Heath. If the house party and the drunken excess of his friends didn't work, Drew wasn't sure what else to do.

"I'll make a menu, Mr. Sinclair. Nothing too fancy, mind you. Roasted chicken. Duck. Possibly lamb. I can see if Dobbins will do some fishing. There's trout near here."

"That will be fine, Mrs. Ebersole. A gentleman from Horncastle will be making a delivery tomorrow. Wine. Possibly some brandy. It seems you can't get good Irish whiskey in Horncastle."

"Mores the pity," Mrs. Ebersole snorted. "Drink something else."

Drew ignored her. "I'll assume there is a root cellar or another place where such things can be stored."

A grunt was her only response before she bustled off.

He would *never* win over Mrs. Ebersole.

Chapter Twelve

Arrogant. Conceited. Condescending.

There was an entire list of words to describe Sinclair's character.

Hester made a list as she trudged up the rise to check on first the sugar beets, then the turnips, the cabbages and finally her potatoes. The plants in the smallest field were struggling, their leaves showing telltale lesions of yellow and white. She would instruct Dobbins to cut off anything with a hint of yellow. They might still be able to salvage some of the field.

Clenching her hands, Hester went off to walk about her cabbages and turnips. The hillside before her was dotted with sheep. A small herd, but all hers. The sugar beets were hers. The tiny field of barley stretching beyond the sheep. The bees were hers.

Hester's eyes filled with tears though she refused to allow even one to drop.

Blackbird Heath was *hers*, not Andrew Sinclair's.

It was unfair, an ironic twist that the very man trying to take her home was the only one she'd felt the slightest attraction to in years. There had been a brief flirtation with the son of the butcher before Hester met Joshua, but nothing more than a kiss had passed between them. Then a farmer who she met while searching for a missing lamb. Abel had been his name. But nothing had come of it. Joshua and she hadn't had much of a marriage. Physical relations were at first difficult, then non-existent. The point being, no man she'd ever met before had the effect of Andrew Sinclair.

He made Hester feel as if her blood was on fire, a delicious, dangerous sensation.

And now he wanted to host a house party, at Blackbird Heath. Sinclair was hoping that the onslaught of cards, spirits and filling her house with snobbish accents would force Hester to reconsider her stance. He would strip her larder bare and work poor Mrs. Ebersole half to death cooking for all those people. Sinclair was very much like Joshua, a man who had little care for anything other than his own pleasure.

Hester wandered back towards the house considering the conversation with Sinclair. He'd said two of his friends were financiers, though she wasn't sure what that entailed, exactly. But could she truly ingratiate herself with them and hope they would intercede with Sinclair on her behalf? Convince these mysterious gentlemen that she was a more than adequate land manager and Blackbird Heath a sound investment? Or at least not sell it, for the time being.

If nothing else, she might buy Martin additional time to overturn Joshua's will.

Mind made up, Hester decided to visit Horncastle. She could hardly greet these guests of Sinclair's in her work clothes. Horncastle was not a place she cared to visit, but the current situation merited a trip. A challenge had been issued and Hester meant to meet it. Running up the stairs to her room, Hester donned her next best dress, which wasn't saying much, washed and pinned up her hair before descending once more.

Hester stopped only to inform Mrs. Ebersole, who thrust a bonnet into her hands, that she would return before nightfall.

SMOOTHING DOWN HER skirts, Hester made her way to Godwick & Sons before returning home. The dressmaker had been Hester's first stop in Horncastle. Mrs. Tartt was an excellent seamstress and didn't ask too many questions, namely why Hester, who never left Blackbird Heath, would want to purchase a fine gown. Luckily, Mrs. Tartt had a suitable, ready-made frock available, one which would require only a few minor alterations to fit Hester. After visiting with Martin, she would pick up the gown.

Hester hated to part with so much coin on what she considered a frivolous expenditure, but if there was an opportunity to secure Blackbird Heath, she meant to take it. A good, initial impression on Sinclair's friends was crucial and the gown would help her accomplish that. There was little that could be done for her work-roughened hands save gloves. The freckles sprinkled across her nose would require a bit of powder.

Another expense.

But Hester was determined to do whatever necessary. Even allow liberties with her person if it came to that. Blackbird Heath was that important.

Martin saw her just as she was about to knock, greeting her with a confused look. "Mrs. Black," he said, waving her inside. "Did we have an appointment?"

"No," she answered. "But I was in Horncastle and thought I might drop in, if you've time to see me."

"Of course." A smile appeared below his mustache, making him appear much less the stern solicitor and more her friend. Her only friend.

Martin was an attractive man with his sandy hair and blue eyes and for a moment, Hester wondered what her life might have been like if she'd met him and not Joshua Black. Her eyes landed on the small miniature at the corner of the desk of Ellie Godwick, Martin's wife. Her elegantly blonde features stared back, dainty chin lifted.

Ellie Godwick didn't care for Hester. She was far beneath Ellie socially as the daughter of the town sot, a man often found passed out face down in the mud and smelling of gin, that it would be ridiculous for someone like Ellie to be her friend. Martin's wife was from a prominent family in Grantham and well-connected.

"You rarely come to Horncastle, though I'm pleased to see you," Martin said.

"I—had a few things to attend to." Hester perched herself on the settee in Martin's office.

"How is Sinclair?" A hard look came into Martin's eyes.

"Throwing a house party for his card playing cronies at Blackbird Heath." Hester looked away for a moment. "His guests arrive tomorrow from London."

Martin gave her an appalled look. "You must stay here, in Horncastle. I'll find you a room to let for a few nights and—"

"Absolutely not, Martin. I will only leave Blackbird Heath for the amount of time it takes to come to Horncastle, and no more. Anything else will be viewed as more permanent and Sinclair will take it as a sign to sell Blackbird Heath." She shook her head. "I refuse to abandon Mrs. Ebersole and the others."

"I know." He ran a hand through his hair. "Your loyalty is admirable, Hester. But there is something I need to say to you, if I may."

"Of course." Martin was going to tell her that there was absolutely no hope of overturning Joshua's will, something she'd been dreading for weeks. She should have known that trying to find a judge to hear her out was nothing more than a fool's errand. Hester clasped her hands, preparing herself to hear the worst.

Martin took a seat beside her on the wide settee instead of taking the chair across from her, as he usually did.

Hester's brow furrowed as Martin's fingers closed over hers.

"It is more than admiration I feel for you, Hester. Surely, you've realized as much." The blue of his eyes shone brightly in the room before he leaned over, lips hovering near hers.

Shocked, Hester turned her chin so that Martin's kiss landed on her cheek. She'd been prepared for disaster, not a declaration of affection. Pulling away her hand from his, Hester stood and walked a few paces away. "You are my solicitor, Martin."

The smile on his lips faded. "I could be more if you would only allow it."

Hester wasn't sure how to respond and could only stare at the man who'd been her friend and solicitor since the death of her husband. She'd assumed Martin cared something for her, of course, but not—

"Is it because of Ellie?" He ran a hand through his hair again, then smoothed down the ends. "What am I saying? Of course, it is." Martin gave her a pleading look. "I'm sorry, Hester. Truly. I've not been myself. I beg your forgiveness. If you don't wish me to continue as your solicitor, I'll understand."

Hester's chest tightened, though she only went so far as to place a comforting hand on his shoulder. "I think that Ellie's continued illness has been difficult on you."

"Incredibly." The blue of his eyes was filled with remorse. "I don't know what I'll do if—the worst occurs. Ellie had a bad spell last night. I know that isn't an excuse for my behavior, but I hope you can forgive me."

"I do forgive you." Martin was only lonely. His entire life revolved around Ellie and Godwick & Sons. "I know you didn't mean anything by it." She smiled down at him. "We are all guilty of behaving out of character when burdened with such challenges. Ellie will be well once more. I'm certain of it."

Martin nodded. "Thank you, Hester. I don't know what came over me." His usual pleasant expression was once more firmly in place. "Now, we were discussing that uncivilized cur, Sinclair, and the intolerable house party he intends to host at Blackbird Heath. Let us move on from my moment of madness," he cleared his throat with an awkward chuckle. "I have been unable to find a judge to legally remedy your situation, but there may be other means of ridding you of Sinclair." His lips beneath the artfully styled mustache thinned into a cold smile.

Something oily spilled across her stomach, a sensation of not-quite-rightness in Martin's tone.

A bark of laughter came from him. "You should see your face. Dear lord, Hester. I don't mean anything nefarious; I assure you. I am going to seek the help of Bishop Franks, in Lincoln. He was a close friend of my father's and can be influential when the right cause makes itself known. At least, he has in the past. You are a pitiful widow." He winked. "In desperate need of assistance. At least, that's what I will relay to Bishop Franks."

"Oh." A relieved sound escaped her. "Yes, feel free to make me as pathetic as you must as long as the good Bishop renders his aid."

"I plan to tell him you are subjected to Sinclair's whims and often go about in a state of weeping due to his demand you abandon your home. I may include a vague assertion that Sinclair took advantage of your sick, elderly husband. He is a gentleman steeped in deceit, gossip and sordid affairs." Martin grew serious. "I remain hopeful. I won't give up, Hester. Blackbird Heath belongs to you."

Hester nodded in agreement, though she wasn't at all certain Bishop Franks and his connections could be induced to help her. "I've taken up enough of your time, Martin. I should be going. I don't want to be on the roads after dark."

"Shall I escort you back?" His tone was grim and full of resolve. "I have half a mind to confront Sinclair about his treatment of you."

Again, that distinct sensation of dread swirled inside her stomach no matter how Hester attempted to dispel it.

"There's no need, Martin. I have things well in hand. I promise," she said as he led her to the door.

"When you feel you do not," his tone sent a chill along Hester's spine. "Feel free to call upon me."

Chapter Thirteen

Drew didn't expect Mrs. Black to come down for dinner that evening after their contentious breakfast and he wasn't disappointed. Their earlier conversation meant that any engagement between them going forth would be of a hostile nature. Mrs. Ebersole took out her dislike on him at dinner by making sure that the chicken and vegetable stew contained cabbage.

Drew picked out every piece and laid it on a separate plate.

Thankfully, the stew didn't taste of cabbage. And there was a loaf of fresh baked bread and butter. He took his meal into the study, planning to open a bottle of wine to enjoy while he worked on the ledgers. The oddly inconsistent ledgers.

Hester *was* careful with her notations. Not a speck of grain or a piglet escaped her accounting. But she was less careful in regards to the sums noted as profit, but Drew was beginning to expect that had been done on purpose. Joshua Black had probably given the ledgers a cursory glance now and again but failed to check the accounting. Blackbird Heath was profitable, but only a portion of that sum was correctly noted. Hester's way of ensuring Black saw the continued income which went to him, but not *all* of it. Which meant he couldn't spend it.

Digging deeper, Drew discovered other errors that Hester had simply overlooked. Small discrepancies in her accounting for expenses. The cost of a bag of grain, for instance, entered correctly in one expense column but not another. These mistakes were not intentional and when added up would reach a tidy sum. He was good at that, seeking out small cracks in a foundation when it was comprised of rows of sums, able to see the detail but also the larger picture. A useful skill, according to his friend Worth. It complemented his friend's strengths which would make their partnership all the more successful.

If the ledgers could be put in order and Blackbird Heath truly made profitable, Hester *could* manage the place for him as long as Drew kept an eye on her accounting methods. But doing so would mean making a smaller investment in the partnership up front.

Or he could just ask Jordan for the funds.

Drew shook his head. *No.* He'd decided on this path and he meant to follow it. Selling the farm rather than keeping it, still made the most sense. Reviewing the accounts was necessary for Drew to determine the value of Blackbird Heath so a price could be set. Scoggins's bid had been good, but he thought it low.

The house grew silent as Drew finished the stew and bread. The wine was a decent vintage and recently retrieved from the basement where an entire crate of the stuff had been discarded. Hester had converted most of the area, once possibly a fine wine cellar, into a bloody storage space for vegetables and canned goods. He'd stepped on a rotted turnip which made a horrid squishing sound beneath his foot. Like a small mouse.

No matter, tomorrow morning, the majority of the basement would be filled with wine, brandy, possibly gin but no whiskey. The man Drew had found in Horncastle hadn't any, though he'd promised to deliver everything else tomorrow before midday.

Stretching his neck, Drew noticed the light outside the windows had disappeared. The moon wasn't out, and no stars twinkled, it was far too cloudy. Pouring himself another glass of wine, Drew allowed himself to consider what would happen if he didn't sell Blackbird Heath.

Because it would mean keeping Hester Black.

His fingers stretched, thinking of the wealth of auburn hair, usually restrained into a tight plait and wound around her head. He longed to see it unbound and spilling over her shoulders. Shoulders covered with peach tinted skin and decorated with freckles. His thumb would trace over the freckles as Hester got on her knees between his legs. He imagined her plucking at his trousers, the tuft of fire between her thighs perhaps the same shade as that on her head.

A soft groan left him as his cock thickened in an instant.

A branch banged against the window of the study, startling Drew from his thoughts. He turned and looked through the glass, but it was impossible to see anything in the darkness. Listening, he waited for the sound to repeat, but all Drew heard was the croaking of the frogs in the pond on the other side of the house.

Closing his eyes, he returned to thoughts of a naked Hester, luscious mouth parted for him.

Her bosom was small, he'd decided, but not sparse. More like a pair of perfectly ripe plums. Her breasts would fit perfectly in the palm of his hands, bobbing gently as she rode atop him and—

A thump outside. This time along the wall.

Reluctantly, Drew allowed the erotic vision of Hester to fade. He didn't think a thief was lurking about outside but only because there was nothing worth stealing in the house. No fine china or silver, but Hester did have a half dozen prize dairy cows in the barn. The animals were valuable. And Hester had taken on a small team of day laborers a few days ago to help with the sugar beets. It was unlikely but not impossible that one of them was bent on mischief. They might assume Hester was here alone in the house with only Mrs. Ebersole and Mary. Dobbins and Jake had quarters on the other side of the barn.

Drew slid open the side drawer of the desk. He'd taken over the study in the last few weeks, informing Hester he needed a space to work when he actually planted himself in the study to annoy her.

Which it had. The drawer opened to reveal the loaded pistol he'd stashed after the incident in Horncastle. Just in case.

Pulling out the weapon, Drew shut the drawer and slipped out of the study. It could be nothing more than a feral dog. A fox, possibly. Eager to get at King George and his harem.

He'd grown rather fond of King George.

Striding down the hall, Drew made his way outside through the back door to creep along the side of the house. He looked up at Hester's window, but it was dark. Except for the frogs in the pond, the entire farm was silent. The wind blew through the wisteria clinging to the stone of the house, brushing along his arm, but there was little else. Perhaps he'd had too much wine.

Drew lowered the pistol, peering into the darkness.

The grass behind him rustled with purpose.

He spun about and fell to the side mere moments before the blow meant to crack his skull open, fell to his shoulder instead. The force of the blow dropped Drew to his knees. His fingers struck the grass, the pistol slipping from his grip. Any doubts he might not have been targeted in Horncastle disappeared. Drew had been deliberately lured outside. Someone had been watching him through the window, waiting for the rest of the household to fall asleep.

The second blow landed on Drew's jaw, snapping his head back.

The assailant grabbed his right arm, twisting it and attempted to push him to the ground.

A grim smile pulled at Drew's mouth. The one thing he'd learned while engaging in numerous brawls was that he was often underestimated. His appearance often led others to believe he didn't know how to fight. Then there was the matter of Drew being left-handed.

And he was not about to be beaten to death on his own bloody property without having tupped Hester Black.

Drew swung up and to the side with his left fist, popping the shadowy figure of the man who held him, on the temple. Again and again,

Drew struck, until the man's grip loosened enough for him to break free. The light coming through the window from the study caught on something in the grass. The pistol.

The assailant let out a pained groan, shoving Drew into the house and against the uneven stone.

He tried to make out the man's features, wishing the moon would peek through the clouds or that those blows hadn't made his vision blurry. He held up the pistol, wiping at the blood dribbling from his lip. "Get off my bloody property. Now. Unless you want a hole in your belly."

Malcolm always said a stomach wound was a horrible way to die. Slow and painful.

The man made a sound and sprinted into the darkness towards the pond, and Drew allowed him to go. What else could he do in the middle of the night? Ride to Horncastle for a constable?

The door banged open. A pale hand held a lamp aloft, the light sliding over Hester's features. "Who is out there?"

Drew's head ached something fierce.

The light spilled around him. A small gasp came from her. "Mr. Sinclair?" Hester hurried into the grass, the white of her nightgown flapping about her ankles. "Whatever has happened?" She rushed forward, the thick rope of her hair bouncing over her shoulder.

"There was a noise outside the study window. I thought maybe a fox was trying to get at King George. Or one of your cows." He decided not to tell her a stranger had been wandering about Blackbird Heath. Not yet, at any rate.

"You're bleeding. Come, let me help you inside. Did you fall? It's quite dark out here with no moon." She helped him to the open door, holding his arm as she took him to the study and pushed him into a chair.

Drew sat with a plop, wiggling his jaw back and forth. His shoulder was bruised and his head ached, but otherwise, there seemed to be no lasting damage.

Hester glanced at the wine on the desk before leaning over to sniff at him, which gave Drew an excellent view of her perfect little bosom when the cotton of her nightgown gaped open. He could barely make out the color of her nipples in the muted light. Pale pink.

Murderous pale pink.

She straightened. "Let me get some warm water and a cloth." Hester disappeared out the door leaving Drew to his unwelcome thoughts. Not about her nipples, those were entirely pleasant. More the consideration that Hester had decided to stop putting snakes in his bed and placing rooster droppings everywhere and instead chose to rid herself of Drew in more dramatic fashion.

Hester returned, bringing with her a small bowl of water and a cloth. She dipped the rag and proceeded to dab at his lip, wiping at the blood. She was so often wearing a faded dress or a pair of old men's trousers, covered in dirt, and smelling like it, that Drew was surprised at the light floral scent mixed with warm woman coming from her. Bathing soap. Hester wasn't the sort to wear perfume of any kind.

The cotton of her nightgown dipped once more, showcasing a pair of taut nipples and sending an ache down between Drew's thighs.

Having nearly been murdered, possibly by Hester, hadn't dispelled his desire for her in the least.

If she were inclined to look down, she would see the thickness of his cock tenting the crotch of his trousers. A strand of copper fell over her cheek, tempting Drew to wrap the tendril around his finger and pull her closer.

"Mrs. Black." Drew's fingers circled her wrist.

HESTER INHALED SOFTLY at the touch of his skin against hers. The brush of cotton along her nipples reminded her that only a scrap of worn nightgown separated her from Sinclair. The heat of him gently caressed the skin of her chest and throat, rising to color her cheeks.

She did not pull away.

The thumping along the wall of the house had awoken Hester from a sound sleep, one she dearly needed after the events of the day. First Sinclair's declaration of war by announcing his house party and then Martin nearly kissing her. She'd had a cup of chamomile tea and gone to bed.

Hester had blinked the sleep from her eyes and gone to the window, surprised to hear the sounds of a struggle outside below and worried over the hens and King George. There had been recent signs around the chicken enclosure that some predator had been lingering about. Hurrying down the hall, she'd paused to take the light on a table at the top of the stairs before making her way to the back of the house. The study door had been open. A lamp lit on what was once her desk, the remains of a meal and a bottle of wine set atop.

Had Sinclair stumbled outside after drinking far too much wine?

She had hurried out the back door, wishing she'd thought to grab a weapon of some sort. A knife. Or even that bottle of wine sitting open in the study. Once outside, she'd been surprised to find Sinclair, bleeding and wobbling slightly against the side of the house.

"What were you doing up at this hour, wandering about in your nightgown?" he said softly.

Their lips were barely inches apart, so close his breath mingled with hers. Hester's gaze dropped to the sensual curve of his mouth, seeing just a spot of purple and had the strangest urge to touch the bit of wine with her tongue. The mossy gaze caught her staring at his mouth.

Hester could drown in all that green, like an endless meadow of late summer grass.

"I—a thump against the side of the house woke me," she answered. "I found tracks around the chicken enclosure the other day. A fox, probably. But I worried for King George and the hens. I thought I could frighten whatever it was, away."

"In your nightgown? Barely clothed? His eyes dipped to her breasts, the heat flaring in their depths unmistakable.

She gasped as Sinclair tugged on her wrist, pulling her closer until Hester was nearly on his lap. Her heart skipped inside her chest as his beautiful mouth met hers.

Oh.

Not a kiss, but more a caress across her lips. Soft. Coaxing her to kiss him back.

Hester tumbled into his lap, the tips of her breasts pushing impudently into his chest until the sensitive tips pebbled. A soft whimper left her as the sensation lazily floated down to settle between her thighs. His tongue trailed along the seam of Hester's mouth, tasting of wine and sin, sending a quiver down to the base of her spine.

One big hand cupped the line of her jaw, thumb teasing gently at the curve of her cheek. Another sound left her, this one of utter surrender as she melted into his warmth. Hester could hardly believe that this beautiful man was kissing her.

She wiggled on his lap.

And wanted her. His desire was poking her in the bottom.

His free hand moved up the length of her thigh, pausing only to press the pads of his fingers into the flesh. A growl left him and he pulled her tighter, before slowly moving up to cup her breast. Rolling and testing the weight of the small mound, his fingers toyed with the edge of one nipple until a sigh left her.

The place between Hester's thighs grew slick, the need to press her naked body closer to his taking up a steady, unrelenting rhythm inside her. She knew what lie beneath the shirt clasped in her fingers. All of it glorious. Her mind had stopped working properly, slowing under the sensual assault of her body.

Hester's eyes flew open in surprise as he pinched her nipple between his thumb and forefinger, the pleasurable sting making her back arch.

Which was when she caught sight of the ledgers open and strewn across her desk.

Instantly, Hester pushed away from Sinclair, shaking away the muddled haze of sensuality he'd woven about her. She slapped at the hand still on her naked breast.

My God. I was ready to let him bed me.

"Calculating my worth, are you?" She hopped from his lap clumsily, tossing the wet rag at his chest. Horrified at what she'd almost done. This was Andrew Sinclair, the man who was determined to sell her home. That is all Blackbird Heath was to him, a pile of money waiting to be wasted on a wager on some stupid horse at Newmarket. Or the turn of a card.

"Reviewing the ledgers, which I have a right to do since," his voice raised slightly, "I own Blackbird Heath. Until I don't." His anger matched her own. "Isn't that right, Hester? After all, I was just nearly bludgeoned to death."

She drew in a furious breath. "Bludgeoned? You've had too much to drink, more likely and ran into the side of the house."

Sinclair raised a brow. "I did not bludgeon myself against the bloody house. And I'm not foxed. I merely find your timing to be convenient."

Hester's eyes widened. "If I were seeking to *bludgeon* you, Sinclair, I would not miss. I doubt I'm the only enemy you've made since coming to Horncastle."

"Enemies?" Sinclair's seductive gaze dropped to her mouth once more. "I thought we were starting to work out our differences."

Could a person's head explode, merely from being taunted? Hester had to restrain herself from slapping at the smirk twisting Sinclair's lips.

"We are certainly not friends." Hester whirled on her heel. "Nor anything else." Her entire body still pulsed from his touch, aching and raw. Lips still swollen and tingling from the magnificent claiming of his. Her own loss of control was terrifying. He would have only had to lift her nightgown and Hester would have cheerfully bedded him.

And she'd thought selling Blackbird Heath was the worst Sinclair could do.

Chapter Fourteen

"Sinclair." Worth hopped out of the carriage and onto the gravel drive to stand before Drew. "So, *this* is Blackbird Heath." He nodded slowly. "Quite a bit more than a farm but less than a complete estate, I think." Turning around, his friend took in the fields spread out on either side. "I was expecting something more rustic but with more servants."

"I'm happy to disappoint." Drew shook his hand. "I'm glad you could come, Worth."

Mr. Charles Worthington was the second son of a viscount, cheerful in the knowledge that his staid older brother had inherited the title and left Worth to do as he pleased. He was brilliant, cultured, and a devil where women were concerned. Something he and Drew had in common. But Worth also possessed a keen sense of business, unfailingly able to discern whether an opportunity had enough value to invest in.

"My pleasure," Worth sniffed the air. "I never pass up an opportunity to play cards with you, though I am usually the one losing. There is also the temptation of cows. Sheep. Rolling fields of barley. Or turnips. I can't really tell from here." Worth once more glanced at the fields and took a deep breath, nose wiggling in distaste. "Good lord, fresh air. I'll be longing for the smell of soot within the hour, I warrant. I brought Phalen with me, and Grout as you requested."

Two slightly rumpled gentlemen exited the carriage, one with a cloud of brandy hovering about his shoulders.

Phalen, pencil thin with a host of sharp cut angles and a blunt personality to match, stuck out his hand. "Sinclair. Good to see you, though I'm not sure why we couldn't have played cards in town like civilized people."

Phalen was born and bred in London, the son of a prominent businessman who dabbled in exporting. He and Worth had attended Harrow together, as had Grout.

Grout resembled a barrel more than a human being. He hiccupped at Drew, enveloping him in a cloud of brandy. "I don't care for travel, as a rule. I made an exception for you, Sinclair."

"Good to see you both." He shook Grout's hand and clapped Phalen on the shoulder.

"Oh," Grout reached back inside the carriage, features crinkling in adoration. "We brought Lady Downing."

Damn it to hell.

"Splendid," Drew said, casting a look at Worth who pretended to study the pond in the distance. The very last person he wanted to view over a hand of cards was his former lover. Worth had said Grout was pursuing her with limited success. "I wish Worth had let me know. I'm not sure Lady Downing will be pleased with the accommodations."

Worth waved a hand and lit a cheroot.

A slippered foot clad in red velvet came out of the carriage, followed by a voluminous swirl of crimson skirts trimmed in black jet. A gloved hand stretched out for Drew to take as a fog of thick perfume enveloped him.

Only Constance would wear crimson velvet for a trip to the country.

If Drew could have packed her back into the carriage and sent her back to London, he would have done so. Her presence among them was not unusual, but it was sure to cause trouble. Black eyes, like bits of polished onyx, took him in, a sly smile on her rosy lips.

"Andrew, you don't mind that I've joined your little party, do you?" The ebony curls framing her heart-shaped face swayed as he helped her from the carriage. "I didn't even tell Worth I was coming until the carriage came to collect me." She cast a gaze at Worth who shrugged. "You adore surprises, at any rate."

He did not. Surprises were often unpleasant and led to other, more disagreeable things. But the worst part about the appearance of Constance was Drew's utter lack of desire for her. Constance was stunning. Far more beautiful than Hester and much more agreeable.

His bloody cock didn't even so much as rise to greet Lady Downing though it knew well the delights to be found in her bed.

Damn.

"Do I, Lady Downing? I thought you didn't care for the country."

"Neither do you." She held out her hand for him to take. "But yet you haven't returned to London, so I wished to see what was keeping you so amused."

Drew had broken off the brief affair with Constance a few weeks before he'd come to Lincolnshire. They'd met over cards at a ball given by Worth's brother, the viscount, and became lovers that same night. Constance was snobbish, well-bred, and horribly spoiled, something Drew had little patience for. When he ended things, Constance had thrown a chamber pot at his head. One that had yet to be emptied.

"There's little amusement in farming," Drew shrugged. "I'm more assessing the value of the estate at present."

"Oh, yes." Constance gave a little flip of her wrist as she leaned into him. "The venture with Worth. I know you don't want to go to your brother. I could lend you the sum, Andrew."

Yes, but the cost would be quite dear, Drew surmised. He'd be nothing more than Constance's lapdog.

"I appreciate the offer," Drew said, making his meaning clear that he wasn't interested in either Constance's money or rekindling their physical relationship. "But I must decline."

Constance pouted prettily. "You might change your mind."

"Doubtful."

Worth watched the exchange with mild interest. "Shall we go inside? I confess I'm curious about the accommodations at your farm, Sinclair."

Constance's nose wrinkled. "I smell something disagreeable."

"Manure, I believe." Grout took her arm, more for support than anything else. "Allow me to lead you inside."

"Indeed, it is," Drew answered.

Dobbins stood just to the side of the house, waiting for Drew's signal to help with the unloading of the coach. Hester had protested, stating she needed him to go to Horncastle for chicken feed, but Drew insisted.

The driver hopped down; no doubt grateful for the assistance of Dobbins in unloading a large trunk from atop the conveyance. Constance's, no doubt. The trunk sat like a small mountain next to the three valises the men brought for their short stay.

Constance waved at Drew, laughing merrily as Worth came to help her with the stumbling Grout. She paused to give him a seductive look before moving inside.

Hester, in her plain cotton nightgown, with dark copper dancing along her cheek, flitted before his eyes. The sounds she'd made as he kissed her, revealing the passionate nature trapped inside the strident, unrelenting shell she presented to the world. He'd been undone last night after she fled the study, wanting nothing more than to take her to bed. It might be the only way Drew would ever have the last word.

What the hell has happened to me?

Mrs. Ebersole, dour as a bloodhound who'd lost the scent of a rabbit, greeted them at the door.

"Mrs. Ebersole," Drew said to the housekeeper, glancing behind her to see if Hester was nearby. "Is Mrs. Black available? I should like to make introductions." The entire point of inviting his London friends to Blackbird Heath was to impress upon Hester what she could expect in the future should she not relent and vacate the premises. He'd thought her anger at him, both for the kiss and the house party, would prompt her to at least snarl at him and his guests from the parlor.

"The potato fields." She took in Constance with a sniff of disbelief. "Don't expect she'll be back for some time."

Drew gritted his teeth. Hester had deliberately made herself scarce. Well, she had to come back sometime.

>>><<<

GOOD LORD.

Hester glanced in the direction of the house, the raucous laughter emanating from a table set up next to her kitchen garden lighting the air. Not content to stay indoors on such a lovely day to play cards, they'd stomped Hester's rosemary and dill while playing games and swilling spirits. The vehicle conveying Sinclair's friends to Blackbird Heath arrived hours ago, yet Hester had so far declined to make an appearance. She was in a foul mood. Not only because of this stupid house party Sinclair had foisted upon her but because he'd kissed her and taken liberties.

A sigh left her.

Shamefully, Hester had allowed both.

It wasn't only the strangers flitting about her garden and house that kept her away.

Hester had not had a great deal of affection in her life. Certainly, no physical closeness though she'd been married. Until the intimacy she'd experienced with Sinclair the previous evening, she'd no idea how much she craved the touch of a man. His hand had cupped her breast. Toyed with the nipple in such a way that the memory alone had Hester aching between the thighs. She wondered if that was the next tactic Sinclair would take to get rid of her.

Seduction.

Hester shook her head and headed in the direction of the barn.

A feminine, high-pitched giggle lit the air.

She even sounds snobbish while laughing.

Sinclair's band of merry card players also included, much to Hester's surprise, a woman. A shockingly beautiful one. Poor Mary, the kitchen maid, had been pressed into service as lady's maid for the duration of the woman's visit, while one of Mary's sisters helped Mrs. Ebersole in the kitchens. Crates of spirits now sat in the basement, pushing aside all of Hester's careful stores of parsnips, turnips, carrots, and the potatoes that hadn't yet gone to seed, along with a few precious jars of tomatoes.

This ridiculous house party of Sinclair's was costing Hester a small fortune. If he continued to invite his friends too often, he'd bankrupt Blackbird Heath within a year. No wonder he'd been poring through the account books. Searching for every bit of coin he could command. Hester had grown accustomed to carefully hiding some of the profits when Joshua was alive and thankfully had continued to do so. She hoped Sinclair hadn't noticed.

The woman laughed once more, deep and sensual, the sound floating to Hester along with the breeze stirring the grass.

Was there no escape?

She strode into the barn, settling herself atop a small three-legged stool she used for milking. Her scheme of convincing one of Sinclair's friends to help her keep Blackbird Heath now seemed ludicrous after peering at the group through the bushes surrounding the garden. The gentlemen were well-dressed and the woman, a lady. Nothing short of glorious, dressed in crimson with jet dangling from her ears.

The idea that Hester Black, work-worn hands and unspectacular bosom, charming any one of the gentlemen in the garden, was mad. Her deficits in both appearance and breeding were glaring when placed next to that gorgeous creature stomping on the poor thyme and parsley. The gown Hester had purchased with such hope and determination yesterday now seemed foolish, for Mrs. Tartt couldn't possibly compete with a London modiste. She should have bought the bat guano being sold for fertilizer instead.

"Or better yet, put the coin aside," she muttered under her breath. "I'm going to need every farthing if Sinclair keeps this up."

She'd spoken at length with Mrs. Ebersole this morning and explained how she found Sinclair, omitting the obvious. The housekeeper was in agreement that Sinclair had likely been in his cups, and if he hadn't merely stumbled into the stone wall of the house, possibly he'd had an altercation with a farmhand, but it seemed unlikely.

Maybe it had all been a ploy to either garner Hester's sympathy to make it easier to seduce her, or start a trail of false accusations which might force her from Blackbird Heath. A shame really, because for the first and probably only time in her life, Hester had felt…desirable. Even though she'd been wearing an ancient nightgown so patched and mended it more resembled a quilt than anything else.

Why did it have to be Sinclair who'd made her feel wanted?

Her lashes fluttered against her cheeks, sighing at the soft, remembered press of his mouth on hers. He was quite good at seduction. Masterful. It was unlikely Hester would survive another assault upon her senses.

She must have sat in the barn, twirling a piece of straw between her fingers for the better part of the late afternoon, because when Hester finally came to her feet, the shadows were starting to lengthen across the grass.

Mrs. Ebersole, flushed with bits of hair stuck to her cheeks, puffed at the sight of Hester approaching the back door. There was no sign of Sinclair and his friends. Probably sleeping off their wine from this afternoon in preparation for this evening's festivities.

"There you are," Mrs. Ebersole wiped her hands on the apron tied around her waist. "Sinclair was looking for you earlier so he could introduce you to his hoity-toity friends. One of them's a lady. A real one. Lady Downing."

"I—saw her behind the house. She trampled on my dill."

"Humph. Didn't care for her in the least. But one gentleman, Worth is what Sinclair calls him. He's the one you should charm, if you mean to bring someone to your side."

Hester had confided some of her plans to Mrs. Ebersole.

"I overheard him and Sinclair talking about investments and some fancy bank in London," the housekeeper said, her homely features becoming worshipful. "Never seen a man quite so handsome. Charming too. He kissed my hand."

"I don't care what he looks like. All that matters is saving Blackbird Heath from Sinclair. I'll approach Worth. Mr. Godwick is speaking to Bishop Franks and asking for his assistance, but I don't think it will help. I must take matters into my own hands."

Mrs. Ebersole's eyes widened. "I see."

Hester looked down at her horribly rough, reddened hands. "Can you have Jake or Dobbins bring up a hot bath for me? Ask Mary to help me with my hair?"

Mrs. Ebersole nodded. "I'll send her up once she's finished with the lady. The gown is lovely. You'll be a vision." She patted Hester's arm.

Hester snorted. "I only want to appear respectable and not embarrass myself before Sinclair's friends. If this Worth can convince him not to sell the estate, I'll be grateful." How grateful she'd be remained to be seen.

I'll do anything.

Chapter Fifteen

Hester approached the dining room with no small amount of trepidation. This was a somewhat desperate gambit, pretending to be something other than what she was, a country farmer. Smoothing down the olive silk of her dress, Hester breathed a sigh of relief she'd allowed Mrs. Tartt to convince her to spend the extra coin. The effect of the elegant gown would be ruined if anyone caught sight of her hands. Hester instructed Mary on a hairstyle, remembering the sophisticated yet uncomplicated chignon Martin's wife, Ellie, often favored. Looking in the mirror before she'd descended, Hester had been reasonably sure she looked her best.

Her fingers trembled against her skirts.

If Hester couldn't charm this Worth into convincing Sinclair to keep her as land manager, she planned to propose Worth purchase the estate from his friend as an investment.

Dobbins rushed out of the dining room, two empty wine bottles in one hand and a tray in the other, containing the remnants of a loaf of bread and a wheel of cheese.

Damn it. She'd been saving that cheddar.

Her farmhand had been pressed into service for the duration of Sinclair's card party, as if he were merely a servant and not her right hand in the management of Blackbird Heath. Unloading their trunks had only been the start.

Yet another irritation for Hester.

"Mrs. Black." Dobbins bowed, his gaze landing everywhere but Hester.

"Dobbins. Don't look so shocked."

"You look," he stuttered, taking in the pale olive silk embroidered with vines. "Quite unlike yourself." He blinked.

"Not ridiculous, though?"

"No ma'am." He hurried off to fetch more wine, leaving Hester to face those inside alone.

"Well," she whispered under her breath. "Dobbins has declared me presentable. Off I go."

Hester lifted her chin, steeled herself and jutted out the small mounds of her bosom, which looked quite appealing in the gown. The dressmaker had also talked Hester into a proper corset, one that wasn't decades old, along with some decent underthings. At the time, she'd protested the expense, but now, much like the gloves, Hester was pleased she hadn't given in to her usual frugality. Her skirts swished appealingly as she twisted the knob, opening the door without bothering to knock.

It was *her* dining room. Or at the very least it wasn't completely Sinclair's. And everyone in it was busy eating and drinking their way through a great deal of *her* hard work.

The room quieted as she entered and gently shut the door behind her.

Sinclair sat at the head of the table, hair shining like well-polished leather in the candlelight. He observed her without a flicker of surprise. Only mild interest danced about in the green of his eyes. His elegant fingers drummed beside his plate in expectation.

Hester turned from him, seeking out the other three gentlemen seated at the table. The outlandishly handsome rake with golden looks that gave him the appearance of an angel had to be Worthington, if Mrs. Ebersole's description was correct.

He met her interest with some of his own.

A barrel-chested gentleman who reminded Hester of a draft horse sat to Worthington's right. He glanced at her but did little else, his attention completely taken by the elegant lady beside him.

The final gentleman leaned back in his chair, narrow shoulders jutting out from beneath his coat. The point of his chin jerked in her direction with a raised brow.

"Who do we have here, Sinclair?" Worthington drawled in a voice like dripping butter. "I confess I am anxious for an introduction." He stood, as did the others.

Sinclair gave her a bored look, which did nothing but steel her determination further. He did not bother to stand.

Rude, scurrilous—

"This is Mrs. Black," Sinclair answered Worthington. "It was her husband who bequeathed this lovely estate to me." He gave an elegant wave, his manner more careless and self-indulged than she'd ever seen it. "Mrs. Black, join us. Please. Worth, would you mind?"

"It would be my pleasure." The tall, golden god pulled out the chair next to him.

"Mrs. Black, this is Mr. Charles Worthington, financier, rake, and terrible player of bowls."

"I'm not really as terrible as all that," Worth guided her to sit. "Your sister is far worse. I've nearly lost a limb to her." He inclined his head. "Mrs. Black."

"Mr. Phalen." Sinclair pointed at the angular gentleman with the pointed chin. "Mr. Grout," he nodded to the human draft horse. "And lastly, Lady Downing."

Grout bowed before he took his seat once more, smiling politely.

Lady Downing's dark eyes slid over her with little welcome. "Oh, yes. You're the widow."

"I am, my lady."

"Lovely gown," she said as Hester took her seat. "Perfect for dining in the country."

What Lady Downing truly meant was that Hester looked quite provincial in comparison to her London style.

"Don't mind Lady Downing," Worthington whispered in Hester's ear. "She prefers to be the only beautiful woman in the room."

Hester's heart gave a flutter at the compliment, whether Worthington meant it or not. She settled with a grateful nod, appreciative of his kindness.

Worthington shot her a wink.

Sinclair made a sound. He was running his forefinger along the edge of his wine goblet, watching her with hooded eyes.

"Allow me, Mrs. Black."

Worth took up the bottle of wine before him on the table, pouring out a glass of the ruby colored liquid for Hester. "A toast. To new friends, Mrs. Black. I think you'll like the wine. It's an excellent vintage."

Mossy green flashed in her direction as Sinclair's gaze lowered to the swell of Hester's bosom. He lifted his glass at Worthington's toast. "To new friends."

WELL, THIS WAS *just bloody splendid.*

Annoyance and arousal mixed unpleasantly inside Drew's stomach, souring the wine as he watched Worth espouse admiration for *his* widow. He had only himself to blame, warning Worth ahead of time that Mrs. Black would attempt to garner support for her ridiculous plan to keep Blackbird Heath from sale and become Drew's land manager. His friend found the idea far less absurd than Drew, which was another source of irritation. Worth pointed out that Blackbird Heath *was* a prosperous piece of property, one which would make an excellent investment. People, especially those living in the great metropolis of London, needed to be fed. You could hardly expect the likes of Constance to grow her own food.

Drew conceded the point. The idea of Constance so much as pulling a carrot out of the ground was preposterous.

Worth had his hand on the back of Hester's chair as she spoke to him, forefinger lightly trailing along her spine.

How had he not seen that Hester had a spectacular, swanlike slope of neck? Delicate shoulders? He'd been so intent on kissing her last night that he'd paid little attention to the rest of her lithe form, save the rosy pink of her nipples.

God, those perfect pink tipped breasts.

Drew took a sip of his wine, gaze never leaving Hester, wanting to taste those tiny peaks. Roll the tips between his teeth. The sheen of the gown made Hester's skin glow, every rustle of her skirts when she shifted in her chair inducing Drew to murder his best friend and future business partner.

Notable, Drew mused, while taking another swallow of wine, how possessive a man could become over a woman he hadn't even tupped. Barely kissed. One he was actively attempting to force from her home. He wasn't even sure he *liked* Hester.

Worth tilted his head, grazing the side of Hester's cheek with his nose. An accident, his friend would protest, if she objected to such intimacy.

Hester did not. She smiled.

Drew gripped his fork tighter. As a weapon, it wouldn't be very useful against Worth, who was good with a sword. Besides, he liked Worth better than either Grout or Phalen.

You could just go to Jordan for the partnership funds.

Yes, he could. It was becoming more apparent by the day that he should do exactly that, but ironically enough, he was as stubborn as Hester. He didn't want to go to his brother.

Part of the coal at Dunnings is yours.

Yes, but that felt too easy. He'd wanted to do this on his own.

Drew growled into his wine. He amused himself by tracing the line of Hester's mulish jaw with his eyes, longing to take hold of the bit of copper dangling from her simple coiffure. He realized that was where she'd been yesterday, off purchasing this dress so she could seduce Worth into perhaps convincing Drew to keep her on as land manager. Or perhaps inducing him to purchase Blackbird Heath himself.

He'd given Hester the bloody idea.

The more Drew considered it, the more likely that was Hester's game. The seduction of Worth, which would present little challenge, to secure Blackbird Heath. That abundance of copper hair would spill over her naked body with those perfect breasts. For Worth.

The goblet of wine in his hand slammed down on the table, sloshing a bit of the liquid over the sides. Inviting his friends to the country had been a terrible idea.

When he first met Worth, Drew had still been at Dunnings, making a decent living playing cards, attending house parties and seducing widows. The pair had bonded during several games of vingt-un, most of which Drew won. He had envied Worth many things over the course of their friendship: his family's wealth. Pedigree. Status. But tonight, he was jealous of the easy way Hester shared a small joke with Worth. She regarded his friend, not with dislike, but true interest.

Even after he'd kissed her, Hester had never looked at him like that.

Another rumble came from his chest. Perhaps he shouldn't have any more wine.

Constance was batting her lashes in his direction, bored to tears with Grout and Phalen and wanting Drew's attention. She posed artfully, displaying her generous bosom. Smiled, promising all sorts of delights.

Nothing moved inside Drew. Certainly not his cock.

Pouting at his disinterest, Constance turned back to Grout.

Hester leaned just slightly in Drew's direction, challenge and determination written all over her striking features. Not beautiful like

Constance, but all the more intriguing for it. And it had nothing to do with the color of her hair. Slender and lithe. Strong. Muscular arms and thighs from days spent in hard work. Hands calloused but hidden tonight beneath gloves. Hester's attractiveness was that of a horse not yet broken because no one had yet attempted to do so.

Drew desired her more with each passing moment and yet, he'd sent her straight into Worth's arms. How far would she go to secure his aid?

The thought didn't sit well with Drew, nor had anything else since kissing Hester last night.

When the simple meal of roasted chicken, potatoes, carrots, and turnip greens ended, the table was cleared for cards. More wine was brought up from the basement and flowed into the glasses strewn across the table.

"Mrs. Black, you'll join us for cards, won't you?" Drew addressed her from the head of the table. It was the first time during the entire meal he'd spoken to her directly. He expected her to decline. Hester had a natural aversion to gambling thanks to her father and Joshua Black.

"I—" Her cheeks flushed. "I'm afraid I've never played. I don't wish to ruin everyone else's evening."

"Don't trouble yourself, Mrs. Black. I'll help you. We'll be partners." Worth inched closer to her. "I'll teach you as we go along." His arm brushed along hers.

Charming bastard. Drew's fingers pressed into the tablecloth.

"You are so kind, Mr. Worthington." Hester shot Drew a smug look. "I accept your offer."

Hester had picked her champion. Worth.

Grout snored softly, his head falling back against his chair.

"Too much brandy," Phelan said from his spot across from Constance, who he regarded as if she were a delicious biscuit he wished to eat. Phelan had always found Constance desirable.

"Grout." Constance nudged him with her arm.

Grout snorted and wiggled his form about, blinking his eyes. "Dear lord. Have I fallen asleep at your table, Sinclair? Apologies. I should probably retire early. The fault of the brandy I imbibed earlier; I fear." He blushed, looking at Constance.

"You are excused." Drew lifted his glass. "We'll carry on without you." Drew liked Grout, though he didn't understand the man's obsession with Constance. He was probably in love with her, which wouldn't end well. Constance, for her part, treated Grout as if he were some sort of a pet. A large bulldog, for instance.

"Oh, Grout, do go up. We'll resume tomorrow." She patted his cheek.

"Thank you, my lady." He stumbled to his feet, stubbed his toe against the edge of the door and bestowed an abashed smile at the room. "Mrs. Black, it was a pleasure."

"Tell me there is a lamp, Andrew." Constance glanced at Drew. "Least he trips and injure himself."

"There is," Hester interjected. "At the top of the stairs. He should have no trouble finding his room."

Constance pulled her attention from Drew, casting an irritated look in Hester's direction. "How kind of you to mention it." Her elegant shoulders rippled gracefully, pushing the tops of her breasts upward and drawing the attention of the men in the room. Drew included. Constance was impossible not to notice.

Hester's mouth tightened into that tight little rosette.

Grout bumped the door again. "Pardon."

Worth leaned into Hester, whispering to her in a low tone until her cheeks pinked. She gave him a shy smile and picked up the cards before her. Nodding to what was in her hand, she looked to Worth for direction.

Drew had the urge to snap something.

Worth's neck, for instance.

Instead, he picked up his own cards and refilled his wine. "Well then, shall we play?"

Chapter Sixteen

Hester covered her yawn with the cards in her hand, trying to blink the sleep from her eyes. She didn't usually drink wine and she'd had more than one glass. Difficult to pretend interest in the game they were playing while she struggled to keep her eyes open.

Worth lifted the bottle of wine seeking to refill her glass. "No thank you, Mr. Worthington. I believe I've had enough."

"Yes, Worth," Sinclair drawled in a raspy snarl from across the table. "Mrs. Black has had *quite* enough. She gets up at an unspeakable hour to perform her chores."

Did Sinclair need to behave so boorishly?

He'd said few words during the meal, at least to her. Mrs. Ebersole had outdone herself and while the dinner might not have graced that of Lady Prissypants' table in London—the woman decried the absence of aspic for goodness sakes. No one liked aspic—Hester found the meal delicious. She only hoped she had time once she awoke in the morning to place a large pile of cow dung at the base of the steps leading to her now ruined garden. That would ruin Lady Prissypants' slippers for sure. You couldn't get dung out of velvet.

Laughter bubbled from Lady Prissypants' lips. "Chores? I do apologize, Mrs. Black. But Sinclair couldn't possibly be implying that you actually muck the stables and the like?" She shivered in horror.

"I do not muck the stables, my lady. But I do milk the cows. Collect eggs. Feed the chickens. But that is before I head to the fields."

Lady Prissypants stopped laughing. "Oh, dear. You're serious. I can't think of anything worse."

Being a useless ornament is far more terrible.

"Who do you think wrung the chicken's neck you dined on tonight, my lady?" Hester inquired politely. "Blackbird Heath does not operate on its own, I fear. Hard work is required to profit."

Lady Prissypants paled at the mention of the chicken. Good lord, where did she think her meal had come from?

"Well spoken, Mrs. Black," Worthington agreed.

"I prefer my wealth to come through marriage." Lady Prissypants finished her wine, gesturing for Phalen to pour her more, which he did without question. "As you well know, Worth. It has been a goal of mine since childhood," she laughed into her glass before taking a sip.

The tale of how the people gathered around Hester's table seemed to start with Mr. Worthington who had known Lady Prissypants since they were children. Apparently, their family estates bordered each other and had once hoped for a match between them.

"Impossible, wedding Worth," she said to Hester. "He's been ruined for marriage, haven't you?"

"Careful, my lady." Worthington's eyes flickered with warning. "I see no benefit to ever marrying, unlike you. Two ancient husbands. I wonder if there will be a third."

Lady Prissypants shrugged. "I've no idea. Only time will tell." Her eyes slid to Sinclair at the end of the table before rising. She strolled towards him and settled in a chair to his left.

King George was less obvious strutting about the hens.

"Tell me about Blackbird Heath, Mrs. Black," Worthington said from beside her.

"I can't imagine you'd find farming to be interesting, Mr. Worthington."

Worthington really was a *most* agreeable gentleman. Handsome. Kind. Why couldn't Joshua have given *him* Blackbird Heath?

"I find *you* intriguing." His glance slid briefly to Sinclair at the other end of the table. "And I find that the best way to learn about various aspects of a particular industry, requires speaking to someone who is an expert. You are that expert, Mrs. Black." He inclined his head, spilling a honey-gold curl across his brow. "I'm not attempting flattery, I assure you."

Worthington *did* find her attractive, if the way his eyes slid to her mouth as she spoke were any indication, but she sensed he was more interested in what she had to say. "Are you gathering information for Mr. Sinclair? As I'm sure you're aware, he wished to sell the estate."

"He's mentioned as much to me. But I'm not sure I agree."

Hester felt a flicker of hope in her chest.

As they played cards, a silly game where Phalen acted as a dealer while the rest of the group attempted to get enough cards that added up to twenty-one, Hester told Worthington about Blackbird Heath. He already knew a great deal about farming, at least from the perspective of a man of business searching for an investment. She could hardly fathom that this elegant man beside her had ever set foot in a potato field. Worth asked specific questions on profitability, crops planted and why they'd been chosen, resources being used, and what sort of funds would be required to modernize the farm to compete with other, larger nearby estates.

"Has Sinclair reviewed your accounts, Mrs. Black?" Worth asked so that only she could hear.

Well, he'd groped her breast. She'd seen him naked. Did that count? Hester bit her lip to keep the giggle from escaping. The wine was having a curious effect on the direction of her thoughts. "Yes, though I—didn't care for his perusal."

"I'm sure you didn't." Worth chuckled softly. "But it is no reflection on your talents, which are obvious everywhere I look, or on Blackbird Heath. Sinclair has a head for numbers which isn't only useful for calculating the odds of a card game or a horse race. He has a knack for seeing patterns. Shifts in the direction of a business that others miss, including me."

Hester glanced at Sinclair who was calmly sipping his wine while Lady Prissypants brushed her bosom against his arm.

"For instance," Worthington continued, drawing her attention back to him. "I was considering the purchase of a well-known textile mill in Manchester; one I had examined with incredible thoroughness." He gave her a sideways glance. "At least, I *thought* I had. Sinclair offered to give their finances a peek as a favor to me."

"Did you purchase the textile mill?"

"No, I did not. Sinclair saved me from making an expensive mistake." He smiled. "It all came down to raw materials and the producers supplying them. Pertinent facts the owner hid within the long rows of receipts in his ledgers. I hadn't noticed it, but Sinclair did. He's quite brilliant at it. Sinclair will make an excellent partner. I identify prospects, he assesses them." He took a sip of the wine. "I'll find another textile mill."

"You and Sinclair are to become partners?" Hester wasn't sure she'd heard him correctly. "I thought he preferred to make his living at cards, Mr. Worthington." Indeed, she assumed Sinclair to be like Joshua, flitting about and earning his living as a gambler.

"Oh, he did, for a time and was rather good at it." He leaned closer, and Hester caught the light sandalwood scent clinging to Worthington's coat. "But that was because of Dunnings, Mrs. Black. I think you are familiar with desperation and what paths it causes you to take. And before you inquire, that is Sinclair's tale to tell, not mine though it is no great secret in London. His family is considered quite colorful." The blue of his eyes twinkled down at her.

Worthington was beautiful. Intelligent. Respectful.

Hester looked down the table at Sinclair. He was deep in conversation with Lady Downing, seemingly oblivious to the tip of her finger trailing down his arm.

Yet he wasn't Andrew Sinclair.

He had mentioned he'd grown up in the country to Hester. She'd guessed somewhere in Northumberland. Offhand, mentioned brothers. A sister. But little else. Certainly not desperation, just a dislike for cabbage.

Worthington noted the direction of her gaze. "Constance and Sinclair have a history, Mrs. Black," he said, but did not elaborate. "I did some research before our arrival to your lovely home. Lincolnshire will soon feed all of England, mark my words. Arable land," he waved his fork. "Loads of it. Rich soil, particularly in this area. Ability to grow a variety of crops. Our discussion has only confirmed that belief."

"I've managed Blackbird Heath quite well. I would like to continue to do so," she said with no small amount of determination. "It has prospered under my care."

"You are a most excellent land manager, Mrs. Black. I am in complete agreement." But Worthington did not give any indication he would speak to Sinclair.

Hester once more looked down the table. Sinclair was frowning at her despite Lady Prissypants' best efforts to distract him with her bosom which even Hester had to admit, was spectacular. It bothered her, all that fawning over Sinclair on the part of Lady Prissypants.

"I think I require some air." She forced her eyes back to the handsome man beside her. "The room has grown stuffy, and I'm not accustomed to wine." She should ask him to accompany her, but the idea of seducing Worthington for Blackbird Heath, no matter how glorious he was, didn't sit well with Hester at present.

Worthington smoothly came to his feet, tucking her hand securely in his arm. "I would like to indulge in a cheroot. Would you mind the company?"

A giggle came from the end of the table. Lady Prissypants was practically in Sinclair's lap.

Just as I was last night.

Hester shored up her resolve. Opportunity was before her. And she wouldn't have to witness such a disgusting display.

"I would welcome it. I would like your opinion on—a proposal for Blackbird Heath. I wish to know if it has any merit." Worthington merely needed a small push in order to rally to her cause. *He* believed in Blackbird Heath. Farming. Knew about the sort of bloody sheep she kept. Perhaps if she allowed him to steal a kiss or—something more—at the very least she was better than Lady Downing. Hester meant to give herself for a purpose. Blackbird Heath. And, she thought, looking up at Worthington, it would be no great hardship. Worthington wasn't the least annoying, unlike Sinclair. He was also magnificent.

"A proposal?" He gave her a bemused look. "I will give you every consideration."

If Worthington couldn't convince Sinclair to leave her as land manager and end this stalemate, maybe she could be *his* land manager. Running Blackbird Heath for a gentleman such as Worthington would be a pleasure.

The wine had filled her with a great deal of bravado.

Sinclair didn't once look in Hester's direction as she and Worthington left the dining room, not with Lady Downing's bosom almost pressed into his face. Why had she even attempted to negotiate with him?

Is that how I'm going to refer to the kiss we shared? A negotiation?

No, that had been something else entirely.

Heat floated over her cheeks and along the curve of her neck, recalling the way his mouth had taken control of hers. The warm cedar scent emanating from his skin. The play of muscles along his chest and shoulders. All of which had been put on full display as Sinclair handed her back the poor garden snake.

The mere memory had her nipples tightening into buds beneath the silk of her gown. The feel of his—

Hester tripped over a rock, but Worthington caught her. "Thank you." She looked up at him, wondering why the thought of *this* beautiful, man naked didn't fill her with—lustful tendencies. It would make things far easier.

Worthington stopped and gently released Hester, walking a few steps to the left. With a flick of his wrist, he lit the cheroot, blowing out a series of smoke rings.

"It's lovely out here, Mrs. Black. I like the sound of the frogs. I thought I saw a pond earlier."

"You did. It's on the other side of those trees." She pointed. "The barns and other buildings are only a short walk away, not near the house."

"Isn't that odd for a farm, Mrs. Black?"

"Blackbird Heath didn't begin as a farm but as a stately manor for a lord who lost his head to Oliver Cromwell."

"Ah. As so many did. They probably danced. Or dressed in a color other than gray. The Roundheads didn't care for such things." Worthington's face remained in shadow.

"My husband's family was awarded the manor long ago, but their fortunes did not improve when Cromwell was gone." She gave a tiny sigh. "The buildings were added later, once they realized they were not on the right side of things after all."

Not exactly the most flirtatious sort of conversation, but Hester was not practiced at seduction. She'd only kissed three men in her entire life.

"Mr. Worthington, I'm not sure if you know the terms of my husband's will—"

"I do," he interrupted. "I find it strange, though I suppose he was trying to satisfy what he considered a debt of honor as well as provide for you."

Honestly, Hester had no idea what Joshua had been thinking, or if he'd considered her welfare at all.

"Then you realize that my circumstances are not ideal. I have no desire to leave my home, nor do I think Sinclair wishes to remain here. We both know he dislikes the country and wants to sell the estate."

"No great secret," Worth agreed.

But," she raised her head to his, prepared to do whatever was necessary. "Would you consider buying Blackbird Heath from Sinclair? Make me your land manager? I know you mean to go into business with him. Perhaps you would consider—"

"Mrs. Black." he held up a hand.

"Discussing the subject further in my chambers," Hester said in a rush before her courage failed her completely. "Where I believe I can better explain the benefits to you."

Chapter Seventeen

Hester and Worth had left the dining room at least half an hour ago, an agonizing stretch of time in which Drew's jealously conjured up a host of scenarios between the pair. The front door had opened and closed. Footsteps sounded. But neither returned to the dining room.

Drew's fingers curled into a fist.

He should have made things clear to Worth upon arrival. Don't expect to be waited on by an army of servants. Don't disparage the simple fare that would be served for dinner.

And no *touching* Mrs. Hester Black.

Of course, Drew hadn't anticipated he'd *care*. Or that Hester would be shockingly lovely in the candlelight and attempt the seduction of Worth. He'd thought Hester would be uncomfortable. Awkward. Instead, she'd charmed his friend and was probably tupping him.

"Andrew." Constance pinched his arm. "You're ignoring me."

He hated when she did that. Whined and pinched his arm. The reasons why he'd ended their affair became clearer with every minute spent in her company.

"Are you even listening?" The seductive, cajoling tone had left her words. A tiny scowl flitted across her mouth. "Worried about your little farm girl and Worth?" Constance boldly ran a finger along his chin. "It was my understanding you had to get rid of her so you can sell this lump of manure."

Drew glared at her.

"What?" She gave him an innocent look. "Worth told Grout who in turn, told me. I suggested to Worth that if Mrs. Black was the least attractive, he could make her his mistress for a time. You know Worth. He's always liked women far beneath him, and I don't mean that in the crass sense. There was that chit he nearly wed. A dull nobody. But I'm not supposed to speak of her." She shook her head. "At any rate, you know Worth. He likes the lowborn. Farmhands, milkmaids, governesses, actresses—"

"You mean like my mother." Constance had always been disdainful of Drew's mother. Yes, she'd been an actress. And his father's mistress before they wed. It was the entire reason most of society looked down on the Sinclairs. But she'd also loved Drew and his siblings fiercely. Adored his father. Mother was so much more than a bloody actress. Her death at Dunnings haunted him.

"You're a snob."

"Andrew Sinclair," Constance teased. "Of course, I am." A pout formed on her perfect lips. "I don't blame you, of course. You can't help it that your mother was an actress. I'm told she wasn't a very good one," she giggled.

Drew turned away, afraid he might do Constance bodily harm.

He thought of Mother, weeping at the death of his father. Her beautiful features contorted with grief. The pitiful violets he'd pressed into her hands after they'd all been banished to Dunnings, hoping to see her smile once more. How she'd hugged him and Malcolm to her chest, trying not to cough as her life ebbed away.

"I was speaking of actresses in general as being low born. At any rate, I only meant that Worth isn't very picky. He enjoys women of all classes."

The floor above them creaked with footsteps. A door shut.

He better not be enjoying Hester.

"I don't think he's ever bedded a farmer," Constance's words slurred just a bit. "I think for the most part because farmers tend to be male. Mrs. Black is unique in that respect. The only thing interesting about her."

"Stop speaking, Constance. I insist."

"You've become incredibly boorish, Andrew. Perhaps I should retire."

"Perhaps you should."

Drew stared at the dining room door, willing it to open and Worth to step inside, all the while ignoring Constance's fingers trailing over him when he wanted Hester's hands on him.

The entire evening had been spent watching Worth attempt to wedge himself beneath Hester's skirts. Flirting and whispering. Making her blush. Asking her questions about farming and Blackbird Heath while pretending great interest. Worth had poured her far too much wine, deliberately getting her foxed so that he could—

"Andrew." Constance pressed herself into his lap. "I apologize and beg your forgiveness for whatever it is that has distressed you."

Drew stood abruptly, nearly toppling Constance from his lap. She flailed about for a moment, before falling back into her own chair. "You don't even know what you are apologizing for."

"I assume," her voice grew thin. "Because you perceive I insulted Lady Emerson. Or possibly that little widow." She sat back as understanding lit her eyes. "You like the little widow, don't you?" Constance laughed. "How rich. Goodness, do you seduce her while she's milking the cows?"

"Shut up, Constance." Drew walked to the door.

She fell back at his rebuke. "You can't be serious. I'm here and willing to forgive you for breaking my heart."

He snorted.

"And you mean to leave me here alone for the remainder of the night, all over *her*?"

"Phalen might still be awake," he snapped, far too concerned about what Worth may or may not be doing to Hester at this very moment to worry overmuch about Constance or her hurt feelings.

"Try his door. But not mine."

Chapter Eighteen

Hester's fingers caught in the folds of her gown, admiring the pattern of vines along the skirts. She had never owned anything half so lovely before. Dresses, of course, most made of serviceable muslin, worn and mended until there was barely enough fabric left for scraps. But nothing like this. Ready-made and sewn by a country dressmaker, nothing at all like the fine gowns Lady Prissypants had. But still, the olive green silk was the most sumptuous gown, the *only* gown, Hester had ever owned in her life. Nothing special by London standards. Still, she loved it.

Even though she couldn't seem to get *out* of it.

This was the reason, she thought, twisting one arm violently over her shoulder. That a lady required a maid. You couldn't get in and out of your blasted clothing on your own. Not with the dozens of silk clad buttons lining your back.

The edge of her finger glanced off a button, failing to take hold.

A bloody good thing she loved this gown because the garment wasn't coming off anytime soon. She'd be sleeping in the blasted thing tonight. Her hands stroked the silk once more, hating that she might ruin such a fine gown. Mrs. Ebersole had already promised to pack it in tissue and carefully store it.

"I'll never wear this gown again. I should just sell it for seed." She spun about once more, giving a cry of frustration as she failed to reach the buttons.

Mary had helped Hester get dressed this evening, buttoning her in the gown with little effort. But the kitchen maid, as well as Mrs. Ebersole, had gone to bed long ago after spending the entire day running about like rabbits in their attempt to satisfy Sinclair's London friends. They deserved a good night's rest before having to once more wait on Blackbird Heath's unwanted guests.

Sinclair and his stupid London friends.

Not being able to get undressed for bed only added to Hester's mounting humiliation. Mr. Worthington had not agreed to her brazen invitation at the pond, preferring not to escort Hester up the stairs. She'd greatly overestimated her appeal and that of the olive silk gown. Now she was left mortified that her actions might have offended Worthington and he would reconsider helping her.

Which he also had not agreed to.

"Ugh." Twisting her arms around the back once more, Hester stretched her fingers, hearing her shoulders pop as she attempted to grab at the row of buttons, spinning around in a circle like a crazed chicken until she gave up once more.

Worthington, far too polite to decline her invitation outright, had wandered off with his cheroot after bidding her good evening. Somewhat humiliated at his rejection, and partially relieved, Hester had made her way up the stairs to her room, careful not to make a sound. She'd listened, cocking her ear as she stood on the landing, for any sound from the drawing room.

The house stayed silent.

Once upstairs, Hester became aware of her situation. At least, she'd managed to rid herself of the petticoats, so that was something. But the corset, a horrid contraption akin to a torture device, was buried beneath the gown. She'd had to take shallow breaths all evening just to keep from fainting.

So much for her brief turn as seductress. It had been a ridiculous plan to begin with. Worthington's looks dictated he could have any woman he wished. A country widow living on a farm would hardly be his first choice. Hopefully, Mr. Worthington, unfamiliar with Blackbird Heath, hadn't fallen into the nearby pond with his dangling cheroot or stepped in a pile of animal dung which would only add to her mortification.

Hester flopped back on her bed, rolling about like a small sausage, the bloody corset barely allowing a breath. She spared a thought for Sinclair, wondering if he was still in the dining room, trapped by Lady Downing's magnificent bosom.

Hester peered down at her own assets.

Pathetic.

Clearly, she was not made to be a lady.

She rolled herself into a sitting position and tore at the pins holding her hair, before flopping down on the coverlet once more. Truthfully, Hester was relieved Worthington had politely refused her advances. He might be the most beautiful man she'd ever seen, but he sparked no desire in Hester. No gentle pulse between her thighs or gentle awareness of his presence.

No, those feelings were reserved exclusively for Sinclair.

Frustrated, Hester rolled to her stomach, refusing to give up. Spinning atop the bed trying to reach the buttons, she considered rubbing herself against the wall. Perhaps that would cause the bloody buttons to snap off and thus free her.

A soft knock sounded at the door.

Hester paused mid-twist and looked up at the door, wondering who would disturb her at such a late hour. Had Worthington changed his mind?

Did she want him to?

Frowning, she stared at the door.

If it was Worthington, and honestly, who else would be at her door at this hour, Hester would politely send him away with the excuse the wine had given her a terrible headache.

But not before asking him to politely unbutton the gown.

Another rap sounded. Louder.

Goodness.

Composing herself, which was difficult given she'd been struggling for what seemed like hours to free herself from the gown, Hester stepped over the small piles of petticoats littering the floor and kicked the matching slippers under the bed. Her hair was down, but she couldn't do anything about that.

Hester cleared her throat and opened the door a crack. "Mr. Worthington—" The greeting died on her lips.

Sinclair stood in the hall, not Worthington. His fists were clenched, the green of his eyes hard and cutting as emeralds.

"Not Worthington," he practically growled, pushing open the door.

Hester stumbled back, her foot catching in one of the discarded petticoats. A wave of physical longing struck her unexpectedly, rippling down her entire body. Her stomach twisted into a delicious knot.

"Sorry to disappoint you, Mrs. Black." Sinclair reached behind him and shut the door, throwing the lock.

Oh. Dear.

Disappointment was the least of the emotions surging through Hester. Her body, every nerve trapped inside this stupid dress, arched in Sinclair's direction while her mind steadfastly maintained shock and outrage at his appearance.

She ignored the instant fluttering between her thighs. "I have retired for the night, Mr. Sinclair."

"Retired, but expecting Worth? Why don't I wait with you for his arrival." He came further into the room, stalking towards her like some great cat.

"Get out," Hester sputtered, keenly aware of him, as she had been all night. "Don't you have your own business to attend to? Lady

Downing and her generous bosom for one. I don't relish the thought of her roaming about looking for you. She might step in something unpleasant."

"Her generous—" Sinclair blinked in confusion, before a slow, lazy grin crossed his lips. "Are you jealous, Mrs. Black?" His eyes flicked downward to her breasts.

"I insist." Hester stamped her foot which wasn't nearly as forceful when you had only stockings on. "That you must leave. Immediately. I've tolerated your foppish antics and your friends long enough. You may own Blackbird Heath, but you do not own me."

They both paused, staring furiously at each other.

Finally, a bemused look crossed his handsome face. "Can't get out of that gown, can you, Hester?"

Her lashes lowered at the sound of her name on his lips. She took a shallow breath, struggling to breathe because of the bloody corset, defeated in every way imaginable by this man.

"No."

Sinclair moved closer, the edge of his nose trailing into the strands of her hair. Without another word, his fingers gently worked the buttons free along her spine, palms spreading every so often over her shoulders and back.

Hester felt every brush of his fingers, arching at the light, careful touch though flames lashed against her skin. She could never have dallied with Worthington, not when Sinclair made her feel like this.

She sighed in relief as the silk finally slipped down her arms.

"Tell me to leave, Hester." The low rasp ruffled her hair and vibrated along her neck.

"But—" She swallowed. "I'll still be stuck in my corset."

A growl left him, low and feral, a sound Hester never imagined such an elegant man would make. He nipped at the side of her neck, the sharp sting sending a pulse between her thighs. Grabbing her roughly around the waist, he pulled her back against him, palm stretching across her stomach.

"Sinclair." Hester wasn't frightened, on the contrary, she had never thought to feel so aroused by a man's touch. Had decided she could have Blackbird Heath, but not this. There was such savageness in him, she could see it clearly now. The same sort of ruthless desperation that lived inside her.

He pushed her an inch away, tearing at the laces of the corset until the unwelcome garment split apart.

She took a deep breath, filling her lungs for the first time this evening. "That's lovely," she murmured.

"Take it off." The roughened sound of his voice, almost angry, struck her. "All of it, Hester. Every stitch."

Hester lifted her chin, blushing furiously, about to refuse, but the look on his face brooked no argument. "I'm not—" She looked up at the ceiling, unsure the sentiment she meant to convey. Not beautiful? Not Lady Downing? No, that wasn't it.

Hester feared his disappointment.

Closing her eyes, she tossed off the chemise, allowing the wisp of fabric to flutter to the floor and faced him, breasts bare.

He took her hands, pressing a kiss to each palm as she tried to pull them from his grasp, ashamed of their appearance.

"Don't," he whispered, before pulling Hester's wrists to her sides. Leaning forward, the warmth of his mouth circled one nipple, eliciting a small cry from her lips. Her back arched, forcing her breast more fully into his mouth as he worshipped and adored that small, tiny peak, sucking and licking until she flailed in his hold.

He pressed her into the bed, naked save for her stockings. Sinclair regarded her through a heavy-lidded sensual gaze, one that had goosebumps erupting across her skin.

A deep unsure breath filled her lungs.

Lips met hers, gentle. A sensual maneuvering that was more dance than kiss before sucking Hester's bottom lip between his teeth, tugging ever so slightly, the sharp sting sending a jolt down between her thighs. His tongue teased and tasted along her lips, nipping at the corners until with a soft gasp, Hester opened beneath him.

He devoured her mouth, exploring in a languid manner, in no hurry to do anything but kiss her. The tips of her breasts chafed against his shirt, and she longed to have him naked beside her. She reached up to thread her fingers through the silk of his hair, wanting him and his glorious mouth and tongue so much closer.

Fingers slowly traversed her skin, tips trailing over the line of her ribs and across her hips. His forefinger slid into the hollow of her thigh, dangerously close to Hester's aching sex. A slow spool of honey pulsed at the apex of her thighs, filling her with need. Physical relations with Joshua had been limited, but there had been a time, early in her marriage, when he'd attempted to please her.

Hester moved her hips, inviting his questing fingers closer, wondering at the sheer decadence of laying naked beneath a fully clothed man while he pleasured her.

A stroke of his finger moved along her slit, gliding over the wet flesh and Hester wanted to weep at the feel of it.

Sinclair moved lower, hooking Hester's leg over his shoulder. A breath blew through the hair on her mound before his tongue touched the part of her which ached so desperately. She pushed her hips into his mouth, thoughts racing at what he meant to do to her, and what she would allow.

Everything her mind whispered.

But Sinclair was in no hurry. He tasted her there as he had her mouth, the pad of his tongue teasing at a sensation building low inside her. The tiny bud of flesh at her core, so sensitive and aching, begged for him. He sucked and licked until Hester thought she might go mad. Every muscle in her body grew taut, as if she would snap in an instant. Her toes curled, heels digging into the muscles of his back.

He stopped, the warmth of his mouth and tongue stilled, leaving her panting, her body tight as a bowstring.

His lips moved, tongue lapping gently once more.

Hester let out a grateful sigh, the sensations once more rippling over her skin.

But again, his ministrations halted. The small bud lodged inside his mouth trapped and painful.

She twisted, trying to push herself off the edge and into the bliss she sensed lying just within her reach.

"I won't beg." Hester breathed, every nerve in her body screaming. She wanted to sob and rail at him. "I won't. You—"

His mouth moved again, sucking Hester into his mouth over and over, the pad of his tongue—

Hester's hips launched off the bed as her pleasure ripped through her, the intensity of which had her seeing stars. She pulled at his hair, tightened her knees, trapping his marvelous mouth firmly between her thighs. Hester had experienced this sensation on a few other occasions. Once, with her husband, and then again on her own, but nothing at all—

Another roll of bliss left her gasping. She turned and bit the pillow to keep from screaming and waking the entire house. Hester's mind went still for perhaps the first time in her adult life. Absolute blankness. She thought of nothing but the feel of his mouth and her pleasure. Not Blackbird Heath, or her crops. The damn bees. She struggled to breathe properly, as the sensation began to slowly ebb from her limbs.

A satisfied sound came from between her thighs.

She looked down to see him regarding her, the green of his eyes contrasting sharply with the tuft of copper hair between her thighs. He took hold of her hip and rolled her to her stomach. Leaning over, he pressed a kiss to her cheek as Hester struggled to regain her senses.

"Stay put."

The sound of clothing being cast off and falling to the floor made its way to her still muddled thoughts. She craned her neck, enough so that she glimpsed a stretch of muscular thigh before he once more loomed over her on all fours, the bed dipping with his weight.

A line of open-mouthed kisses started at the base of her neck and lazily made their way down Hester's spine. He moved over each of her buttocks, nipping at the skin while slowly pushing Hester up on her knees. Tongue dipping once more between her thighs, he teased at her flesh once more until she whimpered. The hard, heated length of him brushed along the back of her thigh a moment before he took hold of her waist.

A single, savage, thrust inside her took Hester's breath away. Joshua hadn't been nearly so large. Her head fell to the bed with a moan.

"Hester," he breathed against her neck and wrapped his fingers in her hair, pulling her head back slightly. He held her so tight, that even had she wanted to get free, she couldn't. His teeth nipped at her collarbone as he started to move, slowly at first, his hips rocking back and forth until she whimpered.

The bed protested as he thrust hard inside her, his hand dropping from her hair to wrap around her neck. He was not gentle, taking her so savagely Hester feared the bed might break. Sinclair took one of her poor worn hands in his, lacing their fingers together.

Every stroke claimed Hester, not just her body, but her very soul.

And she surrendered to it. To him.

His hand moved between her thighs once more, stroking along her slit until Hester's body clasped his tightly.

Every stroke grew more forceful until a groan left him and he took her between his fingers, pinching gently. Teeth sunk into the skin of her shoulder, the sting forcing her to cry out. Their bodies rolled together in unison, Hester finding her release within seconds of his. It was blinding and so very beautiful.

"Drew," she choked out.

DREW PRESSED A kiss to Hester's flushed skin, along the mark he'd left on the slope of her shoulder. Pressing his forehead to her back, he struggled to breathe, shocked at his lack of control. He'd never—*lost* himself in a woman before. Not like that. Like some bloody animal claiming its mate. The pleasure had been so intense, all of Drew's senses had converged upon each other until all he could feel was his cock buried in Hester. He was still inside her.

She stretched beneath him, like a pampered housecat.

Drew gently rolled to the side, keeping their bodies clasped tightly together. He curled around her, hand idly caressing the slim, muscular thighs before reaching for her hand.

Hester stiffened and pulled her fingers away, sliding them beneath the pillow. But she didn't move her body away, only wiggling closer.

"I've already seen them, Hester. Many times."

A shaky breath came from her. "This is different," she whispered.

Drew had done most of the touching, he belatedly realized. Hester had only deigned to thread her fingers through his hair. "I would rather have you touch me than not. I don't care if your hands look like King George's feet."

A tiny laugh came from her. "They aren't nearly so bad as that."

He reached and gently pried her hands from beneath the pillow. She'd allowed him to kiss each palm earlier, probably from shock at his arrival in her room, that there had been no protest.

Pulling on one palm, he pressed a kiss, right over a healed blister.

She sighed into him. Such a peaceful sound. So unlike Hester Black.

Because of him.

When he'd arrived at Hester's door, he'd expected to find Worth. Drew hadn't decided what to do if he did, only that the thought of her bedding Worth was intolerable. Jealousy, so ferocious in nature it had taken him by surprise, and he'd marched to her room.

His arms tightened around her smaller form.

Hester felt like *purpose* to Drew. A sense that no matter his aspirations of the partnership with Worth and his dislike of the countryside, he should be by her side. He knew it didn't make sense. Tomorrow was bound to be awkward. For one thing, Drew's friends needed to leave and return to London after only one night. It had been a stupid idea, anyway, hoping to scare Hester from Blackbird Heath with a house party. Nearly as bad as Hester assuming she could seduce Worth into swaying Drew one way or another on the fate of Blackbird Heath.

She sighed into him; sleek body melded against his own.

Drew pressed another kiss against her temple, unwilling to disturb the peace between them. He didn't want to think about the estate or the choice he must eventually make. What he cared most about at the moment, was the sense of contentment at being here in this house and bed with Hester Black.

Chapter Nineteen

Hester had awoken at the first crow of King George, but so warm and comfortable she hadn't wanted to move, let alone open her eyes. A snore sounded, reminding her she was not alone.

Flashes came to her from last night, most so erotic in nature, Hester didn't dare dwell on them. Silently, she slid out of bed, wincing at the soreness between her thighs and tiptoed over to the basin of water sitting on the dresser. She washed and dressed in the dark, not daring to light a lamp, adamantly refusing to look at the large, naked, *gloriously* beautiful man inhabiting her bed. She wasn't ready to face Sinclair.

Drew.

Not after last night. Perhaps never again. She could simply take up residence in the barn until further notice. *Drew* might be as confused by the previous evening as Hester. It had, after all, been a moment of madness. He might be perfectly content if she lived in the barn going forward. At least until he returned to London.

London. His friends. Worth. Lady Prissypants.

Hester meant to avoid all of them. Especially Worth.

Another snore came from the bed. The sheets were down around his waist, the left side dipping lower to showcase one muscled buttock. Another flash of their naked bodies, twisted together on the bed, had Hester holding on to the doorjamb because her knees became weak.

"Milk the cows," she whispered. "I need to milk the cows."

SOMETIME LATER, HESTER finally arrived at the barn. She'd slipped out of the house, first stopping to speak to Mrs. Ebersole, who was already cracking eggs in the kitchen, no doubt beginning preparations for the breakfast the London guests would require. The housekeeper nodded as Hester grabbed a piece of toast and fled the vicinity, not wanting to be peppered with questions about the evening. Or how she'd managed to get out of her gown without help.

Taking up a stool, she started her work, the chafing along her thighs noticeable. The scruff along Drew's chin had scraped the delicate skin. He'd had his mouth on her, deliberately holding back her release until she—

A soft whimper left her.

Hester leaned her forehead against Tabby's side, fingers stilling on the cow's udders. She had never imagined, nor considered, that physical relations could be so incredibly passionate. Or so wicked.

A blush slid up her cheeks. She'd been terrified that Mrs. Ebersole would guess at what Hester had done and could barely look in the direction of Jake when he greeted her outside the barn. Poor Dobbins had been called from his usual duties to help serve breakfast, so Hester checked on the sheep. Fed the pigs and chickens. The cows.

And through all of it, Hester could think only about Drew lifting both her legs over his shoulders while he thrust inside her.

Hester squeezed too hard on one udder, making Tabby stamp one hoof in agitation.

"Sorry."

She forced herself to think about the smaller of her potato fields, the one with the blighted plants, finally in agreement with Drew's opinion weeks after he'd given it. She only hoped that the rest of her potatoes would survive.

If I touch you just here with my tongue, and place my finger like so, you'll climax, Hester. Shall we try it?

Dear God.

Every filthy thing Drew had said to her last night was burned into Hester's mind. A substantial collection of wickedness leaving little doubt that Drew was as much a gambler as a rake.

Another sigh left her, this one far more troubled.

Hester didn't know what any of last night would mean for her future and Blackbird Heath. Or if it would mean anything at all. And while Worthington had certainly given Hester some insight into Drew Sinclair, he was still her enemy. A gambler. A rake, to be sure. Perhaps his attentions last night had been nothing more than a continuation of the seduction he'd begun the night in his study. Intoxicating her with pleasure—

A *great* deal of pleasure—

So that Hester would lower her guard and he could coax her to leave, thus allowing him to sell the estate. She doubted Worthington would be much help. Possibly Martin Godwick had made some progress. Perhaps Bishop Franks had decided to take up Hester's case, but she didn't feel hopeful. A less stubborn woman would leave. Take the sum offered by Drew and move on with her life.

Hester could nearly feel her heels digging into the floor of the barn.

Her stomach rumbled, growling like a wild animal was trapped inside, reminding Hester she hadn't eaten much at all today but a piece of toast. She hadn't wanted to return to the house, though at some point she must venture back. Jake, if she asked, might bring her something from the kitchen. Hester could sleep in the barn tonight. The hayloft would make a comfortable bed. Drew's London friends would depart in a few days.

"I've never milked a cow before, but I'm reasonably sure you must tug on those dangling things for the milk to come out."

Hester didn't turn from the sight of Tabby's hide, at least not right away. She took a moment to compose herself. "I didn't realize you knew where the barn was located, Mr. Sinclair."

It might have once been true, when he first arrived at Blackbird Heath. But Drew had been taking a much bigger interest in the estate, as evidenced by Jake asking Hester just this morning if Mr. Sinclair planned to walk the field of sugar beets today. He'd been doing so on a regular basis though no one had informed her.

"You have so little faith in me, Hester. Of course, I can find a barn. I managed to find an assortment of sensitive spots on you with my tongue last night, didn't I?"

She felt the heat on her cheeks and cursed it. Looking up at him, she took in the clean-shaven jaw, the tailored coat and trousers and polished boots. Perfectly dressed, as always. "How do you manage to turn yourself out so well without a valet? Surely, you should have brought the poor soul with you from London."

"I've never had a valet, Hester. It isn't so difficult to button a shirt or pull on your own boots. A grown man should be able to dress himself without help. I'm not an infant. The cravat," he gestured to the snowy white silk at his neck. "Now that, took some time. Not at all the same, say, as…taking off a corset." There was a mischievous twinkle in the green of his eyes.

The heat flowed down her cheeks to her neck.

"I do so adore how you blush, Hester. Do you recall, last night, when I put my mouth—"

"Stop." Her hands fell away from Tabby.

He shrugged, the smile still in place, as he strolled back and forth across the barn with interest.

"I take it you've never been in a barn before."

"How little you think of me, Hester. First, I can't find the barn and now you think I've never been inside one before. I thought I had redeemed myself. And would have this morning had you not crept out like some thief while I was sleeping. But to answer your question, I've been in a barn before, though not one as fine as this."

"At Dunnings? Worth mentioned it to me. Is it a place?"

Drew's eyes widened just slightly in surprise, before he smiled again, but this one didn't reach his eyes. "I'm glad I had the foresight to send him back to London. Along with everyone else."

"Even Lady Downing?" Hester asked.

"*Especially* Lady Downing. Though it pains me after—I explored every inch of you with my tongue, Hester." His voice hardened just a bit. "That you would assume I'd allow her to stay."

"You are rather blunt when speaking of such things."

"I like watching you blush." There was something indefinable lurking in his gaze as he regarded Hester. An intimacy shared between them. "And more shocking, Mrs. Ebersole was so pleased to be relieved of my London friends, she *may* have smiled at me. Or she was having a fit of apoplexy. Difficult to tell."

Hester's entire being felt as if a lamp had been lit inside her chest. A glowing, warm sensation that stretched out along her limbs making her fingers tingle. His doing.

Drew paced once more, pretended to examine the stone walls, then returned. "I tire of our continued hostility towards each other. I'll admit, as foreplay, it was immensely enjoyable, but—no longer. We need to move forward in a different manner," he said in a somber tone.

Did that mean he meant to keep Blackbird Heath with Hester as his land manager while Drew returned to London?

I don't want him to go.

The thought of him leaving her in the countryside to resume his life, albeit as Worthington's partner, made her stomach lurch unpleasantly.

Hester jerked up from the stool, taking hold of the pail which was only half-full of milk.

Drew took a step back. "Are you going to throw that at me?"

"And waste all this milk?" She shook her head. "Perish the thought." Hester walked across the barn to deposit the milk. Dobbins would be by in a bit to take the large vat to later be churned to butter. Mary had three sisters who did the churning in return for a share of the butter and cheese.

"Hester."

She emptied the pail and took him in, handsome and beautiful against the light in the barn. When had Hester decided that Drew was important to her? Well before last night, only she hadn't wanted to contemplate what their attraction to each other might become. All she'd thought of for so long was Blackbird Heath.

"I want you." The husky, rich words echoed against the stone walls.

The pail fell from her hands, the bits of milk still left inside spilling across the floor. There was such longing in that simple sentence, one that did not only speak of physical desire. The feeling had been there last night, but Hester hadn't trusted it. She'd been alone for so long, it seemed impossible that now she was not.

"Now is where you say something back."

"Have you ever explored a hayloft?" she whispered across the barn to him.

Chapter Twenty

Hester sprawled beside Drew in the loft while he traced the tip of her breast with a piece of straw. She tried to keep from moaning out loud.

The straw slipped from his fingers, her breast disappearing inside his big hand as he cupped the small globe of flesh. Drew had decreed earlier that Hester's breasts were incredibly sensitive and had begun experimenting to see if she might climax by just a caress atop her nipple.

So far, the results had been unsuccessful but incredibly pleasurable.

The hayloft had become their favorite spot for an afternoon tryst since Drew's friends had departed for London. The barn was often empty in the afternoons and free of prying eyes. The fields surrounding Blackbird Heath afforded less privacy as they'd found out yesterday, when one of Hester's curious sheep interrupted them. No one at Blackbird Heath seemed suspicious of their relationship but they still couldn't simply rush up the stairs to Hester's bedroom whenever the mood struck.

All things considered, the barn wasn't such a bad spot.

There had been no more talk of selling Blackbird Heath, for which Hester was grateful. Nor could she inquire with Martin Godwick if any progress had been made on her behalf with Bishop Franks. Ellie Godwick had died, in Grantham, while she and Martin had been visiting her parents. He still hadn't returned to Horncastle and Hester didn't want to intrude on his grief.

Even if Martin had made progress before Ellie's death, Hester was afraid to ask, unwilling to allow anything to burst the small bubble of happiness she'd found. Her life had been one of hard work and constant worry over things which were beyond her control. Someday, Drew might take Blackbird Heath from her, but for now, Hester relished having a lover.

While guarding her heart.

"I'd forgotten there were some things I like about the country." Drew leaned in and pressed a kiss to one of her nipples, before blowing a breath across the tip.

Hester shivered at the intimate touch.

"I'm happy to know you've adjusted to chicken dung." She bit her lip. "Tell me about Dunnings." The question of Dunnings, which she assumed to be a house or possibly a farm such as Blackbird Heath, had gnawed at Hester since Worthington first mentioned it to her. Now, while Drew was relaxed seemed as good a time as any to ask. "Northumberland, correct?"

His face clouded over, but he answered. "Yes, outside of a village by the name of Spittal, notable only for once having had a leper's hospital, but little else."

"How did you come to be there?" Hester leaned into him, running her hand down the length of his naked body, watching his cock twitch at her touch.

"Naughty girl. I once had an elder half-brother by the name of Bentley. The product of my father's first marriage."

"Had?"

"He's dead," Drew said with a shrug. "I don't miss him. Bentley was a terrible person. It was he that sent us all to Dunnings, a place best left forgotten." There was a hard glint in his eyes, seeing the past.

"Why would he do such a thing?" Hester caught sight of her reddened work worn hands as her fingers trailed along his hip. No matter how much salve she used, or gloves she wore, her hands would always be the least pretty part of her.

Drew absently took her fingers and pressed a kiss to her palm.

A small, insignificant action, but one that spoke volumes to Hester.

"My mother," Drew's voice grew thick. "Met my father when he was already wed to Bentley's mother. Mother was an actress. Trod the boards at Covent Garden. Though I don't think she was talented, only beautiful. She became my father's mistress, then his wife. You can imagine the scandal, Hester. If you think marrying a gambling wastrel is terrible, I can assure you an actress who was once a mistress is far worse. Lots of shaming. Insults hurled at us. My sister, Tamsin, broke the nose of the Marquess of Sokesby. My father had just died. Banishment followed."

"You're joking." Drew's family had been and probably still were, members of society. She hadn't expected that.

"I am not. My mother died at Dunnings." The sadness in that small sentence filled the air between them.

"I never knew mine," Hester admitted. "Not really. She died of the ague when I was three or four. My father was never very clear on that. I remember a soft voice and the smell of violets, but little else." She'd already told Drew about her father, Thomas Morton, though he'd already known. Gossip in Horncastle, she supposed.

Drew's mouth brushed hers in a gentle kiss.

"My mother was—wonderful. Always dressing us up to perform plays. Malcolm and I were often tasked with being sprites or fairies." He gave her a smile. "Mother loved Shakespeare. Tamsin, that's my older sister, blames herself for the banishment because of the nose-breaking incident. Ridiculous. If Bentley could have shipped us to India, he would have. But I suppose Ware will have to deal with the challenge of Tamsin now."

"Ware?"

"Not important at the moment." Drew gave a graceful flick of his hand.

Hester understood now, at least somewhat, his reticence about the country, farms, Blackbird Heath. He associated the country with the death of his mother and the banishment of his family. She felt the same way about card playing and dice. "Is that why you don't like cabbage?"

"The only thing," Drew's mouth moved to the line of her neck, "which could thrive at Dunnings. Certainly, nothing else did. Including the Sinclairs." His fingers dipped between Hester's thighs. "I do adore that your hair is as red here as on your head."

A gasp escaped her as Drew found a particular spot. He remembered each of them, having mapped her body with great attention.

"Dunnings was a pile of rubble when we arrived. No servants of any kind. Not even a cook. Holes in the roof. Drafty and cold. The monthly pittance Bentley sent was barely enough to feed us. Spread your legs, Hester."

A roll of heat curled low inside her at the press of his fingers. Her head fell back. "Drew."

"Don't interrupt. I'm not telling this story again. There wasn't enough for a doctor when Mother became ill. I was only a lad, but I had to do something. I found a dice game in Spittal. Wagered the silver buttons on one of Tamsin's dresses. I won. Next, I tried cards, which I became good at."

Hester whimpered softly, reaching for him.

"Eventually, I caught the eye of an older widow. Unsurprising, I know. And in addition to introducing me to the delights of the flesh—" Drew made a twisting motion with his fingers inside her, and Hester whimpered as a bolt of pleasure struck her. "She also introduced me to wealthy merchants. Landed gentry. House parties."

Hester's breath came in small pants. "You helped support your family." Andrew Sinclair was the furthest thing from a wastrel. And he'd once been wealthy if he expected servants and his sister had a dress with silver buttons to wager. How had she not seen it? Drew wasn't anything like her father. Or Joshua. He'd become a gambler and fleeced a great many gentlemen because he *had* to.

"Alas." There was an edge to his words. "There weren't enough bloody games of whist in all of England to save my mother. And if a carriage accident hadn't taken Bentley's worthless life, I would have."

Drew rolled on top of her, thrusting into Hester with such force, she cried out, praying that no one had wandered into the barn. She could hear the truth of his words. The wound of his mother's death that still haunted him.

"Now you know the truth of Dunnings," he whispered against her lips. "We are more alike than you know."

He slowed his body rocking into hers with exquisitely slow movements, so desperately tender and filled with all the things Drew did not say, that Hester sobbed his name. She clung to him fiercely and vowed to never let him go.

CHAPTER TWENTY-ONE

"Mrs. Black." Mary stood at the bottom of the steps, as Hester descended with a smile on her lips and a tad sore between the thighs. She had never imagined that inside her stubborn, determined chest beat the heart of a passionate woman. There were nights, like the previous one, where she and Drew nearly tore each other apart in their need to be joined.

Hester doubted anyone at Blackbird Heath was fooled any longer. She and Drew did not sleep apart, sharing a bed even on those rare instances when Drew didn't tup her. He had stopped sneaking into his own room when King George heralded dawn was near, because Drew got up with Hester. They often went to the fields together, discussing the upcoming harvest.

He'd stood beside her, holding her hand as the rest of the potato fields were burned because of the blight.

"It's stupid for me to weep over potatoes," she'd whispered to him, wiping a tear from her cheek.

"No, it isn't." He'd squeezed her fingers and pressed a kiss to her temple. "Those were important potatoes."

Hester smiled at the memory.

"Mrs. Black." The maid stood looking at her.

"I'm sorry, Mary. My mind was on the sugar beets. What is it?"

"Mr. Sinclair said to remind you he's gone to Horncastle today to post some letters, in case you are looking for him this afternoon. You were with King George." Mary giggled a bit. "He didn't want to interrupt the royal visit."

Drew had made great progress recently in charming the entire household. Mary and her sisters stammered and turned red whenever Drew was around. Even Mrs. Ebersole had finally warmed to him. At least there was no more cabbage being served.

"Thank you, Mary." Hester turned to go down the hall.

"And Mr. Godwick is awaiting you in the parlor."

"Mr. Godwick?"

Hester had not seen Martin since her last visit to Horncastle and they'd parted so awkwardly. After Ellie's death, Hester had written him in Grantham, expressing her condolences but received no reply. Mrs. Ebersole, who traveled frequently to Horncastle, informed Hester that after Ellie's funeral, Martin had chosen to stay with Ellie's parents.

"Martin." Hester entered the parlor. "I didn't realize you'd returned from Grantham."

He stood, thinner than she remembered. Drawn. Deep brackets had taken up residence around his mouth and smudges of purple beneath the blue of his eyes. Hester's heart went out to him.

A weak smile crossed his lips. "I apologize for not answering your letter. I was—occupied."

Hester took his hand, squeezing his fingers. "Sit. I'll have Mary bring tea." He appeared so stricken, so unlike himself. "I'm so sorry about Ellie. And as far as not answering my letter, there need be no apology between friends." She released his hand and asked Mary to bring them tea and perhaps some of those little biscuits Mrs. Ebersole was now making every day. Drew's favorite.

"No tea, Hester."

Hester belatedly realized that Ellie had sickened after drinking tea. "I wasn't thinking, Martin. Of course, you don't want tea. Something stronger, then?"

"Brandy, if you have it."

Hester nodded and went to the sideboard, pouring them both a small glass. Drew had made sure that the sideboard at Blackbird Heath was well stocked.

"It was a shock, you understand." Martin turned sad eyes to her as she handed him the brandy. "Though I suppose it shouldn't have been, what with her constantly ill. The doctor in Grantham had such high hopes. But I just never thought—" He took a deep breath. "Well, one is never prepared, I suppose."

"No, indeed." Hester gave him a sympathetic look. "Mrs. Ebersole heard you were staying in Grantham for a time. Truthfully, I wasn't sure you would return to Horncastle."

"I don't get on well with Ellie's parents, as you know. And Grantham has never appealed to me. I only wanted to settle her affairs." He sipped his brandy, eyes hopeful. "Would you miss me if I were gone, Hester?"

"Martin, we are friends. You're my solicitor. It goes without saying I would miss you." Hester's fingers pressed into the glass she held, worried if she set down the brandy, Martin might try to take her hand. There was something manic in his gaze as he regarded her.

The brackets at the corners of his mouth deepened, one lip curling until Martin seemed to be sneering. "During my time in Grantham, where I was subjected to the whims of Ellie's parents, I had much time to consider your situation, Hester. I was distressed and shocked upon returning to Horncastle to find that Sinclair is *still* in residence."

"Martin, we have had this conversation before. At least twice to my recollection." Hester took another sip of her brandy, holding the glass against her chest. "You know the terms of Joshua's will as well as I do. I'm sure everyone in Horncastle has been apprised of the situation. If I leave, I lose Blackbird Heath. Plain and simple."

"How cozy you must find it." His tone was ugly.

"There is nothing cozy about being a guest in your own home, which is what I've been reduced to." Outrage laced her words. "I have people who depend upon me. Mrs. Ebersole. Dobbins. Jake. Mary and her family. If I give over Blackbird Heath, where will they go? And this is my home, Martin."

"You realize that the longer this situation goes on, the worse the gossip becomes." Martin leaned back and took a swallow of the brandy, swishing the liquid around his mouth, glaring at her in accusation.

"I doubt anyone cares about the widow of Joshua Black."

"That's where you're wrong, Hester. You've always been a target for rumor given your father's habits and then wedding a man at least forty years your senior. The good people of Horncastle were merely convinced you were merely ambitious and desperate to escape your circumstances, but now the situation has become that much worse."

How incredibly insulting. There was a reason Hester rarely went to Horncastle. Where was the concern of her neighbors when she was starving and dressed in rags with a drunk, gambling father?

"What would you have me do? Beg him on my hands and knees to depart?" she snapped.

Get on your knees, Hester. Part your lips.

A telling flush crawled up her cheeks, forcing her to look away. Pure lust, the sort that would make a woman mad, curled between her thighs, remembering what transpired last night. She'd complied, willingly, with all of it. And would do so again.

Martin's nostrils flared sharply as if he could scent the arousal still clinging to her skin. "Perhaps," he drawled in disdain, "You've grown more accustomed to his presence than you've led me to believe."

"Don't be ridiculous. I find the situation intolerable."

"I don't know if Bishop Franks has heard the gossip, Hester. If he has, you can forget his support."

"There is nothing remotely improper occurring, Martin," Hester lied smoothly. "We are getting on better. I've shown him the fields.

The progress I've made with the bees and sheep. I only want to convince him that I should be left to manage Blackbird Heath while he returns to London. I do not want to leave my home and I see no other solution."

"Hmm." Martin ran a hand through his hair, ruffling the close-cropped locks. "Is he out taking inventory of your crops, then?" There was an odd, stilted note in his voice. "Since he is now interested in his investment?"

"No, he's gone to Horncastle on business, according to Mary. I haven't seen him at all today."

"Perhaps we'll pass each other on the road. Did you know that Scoggins met with Sinclair shortly after his arrival? They discussed a fair price for the property."

No, Hester hadn't known. Drew never mentioned meeting Scoggins in Horncastle. A niggling bit of fear and distrust sunk its teeth into her. The old worry, that Drew was merely seducing her as a means to an end.

Martin turned back to her, eyes like slivers of ice. "It is my opinion that Sinclair doesn't mean to relinquish his ownership of the estate, or its management to you. No matter how *convincing* you are, Hester."

She inhaled sharply. "What, exactly, are you implying, Martin?"

"Not a thing." He rolled his shoulders. "I know you to be a woman of great fortitude." There was only a trace of mockery in his response.

The oily slickness, the sense of dread she'd felt in his office that day in Horncastle, spread out once more across her chest. The sensation was so strong, Hester nearly yelled at the top of her lungs for Mrs. Ebersole. But this was Martin. Her friend. He'd been Hester's rock when Joshua died.

And he'd only just lost Ellie.

Surely, he could be forgiven for his odd behavior. Still, she was relieved to see Dobbins just outside the parlor window when Martin took his leave. But the dread in her stomach didn't ease until long after.

Chapter Twenty-Two

Drew whistled a ribald tune as he left Horncastle, anxious to return to Blackbird Heath and his now *merry* widow.

A vision of Hester flitted before him, her small, perfectly shaped breasts bouncing gently as she rode him to completion this morning. Last night, he'd had Hester on her knees, a wholly erotic sight that still left Drew barely able to breathe properly. Even now, mere hours after he'd last had her, the thought of her sent waves of arousal down his legs. He'd rushed to post the letter to Jordan, who was probably wondering what the hell Drew was doing in Lincolnshire. And he stopped to enjoy an ale with Scoggins, who didn't bother to hide his disappointment that at present, Blackbird Heath was not for sale.

Drew could not sell Hester's home.

He still didn't like the country. Not really. There was too much dust and too many cabbages, but when Drew walked the fields with Hester in the mornings, taking in the neat rows of her turnips and sugar beets, Drew felt proud. Peaceful. A different sort of contentment than he received from winning a game of whist.

So, Drew threw himself into learning as much as he could on crops and animal husbandry. The sheep, or at least their wool, would be worth a tidy sum. Barley should be planted again next year. He'd grown used to King George. But Drew adamantly refused to have anything to do with the damn pigs. Hester was the farmer. Not Drew.

His real contribution to Blackbird Heath would be the management of finances.

The argument that had ensued shortly after Drew had the audacity to point out Hester's mistakes in the ledger and her blatantly incorrect accounting ended with her bent over the desk in the study. She'd screamed out her release over the very column he'd pointed out she'd tallied in error. The pale white of her buttocks and thighs had been spread across the desk. He'd swatted her backside a couple of times, just for his own amusement.

Hester had moaned, pushing her hips at him for more.

Another tingle shot down between his thighs.

Drew planned to review the ledgers with Hester at least once a week.

He had not considered, until recently, that he hadn't been happy in London. The constant whirl of amusements was only a distraction from the anger over Dunnings and the death of his mother. Strange, to realize such a thing after only confessing the truth of his past to Hester. She understood, without him explaining further, what that anger felt like because she'd experienced it herself. An attachment, one long in coming, was forged that day. Physically, they were well matched, Hester being as free in bed as she was staid outside of it. But it was her heart which Drew most desired.

He'd never thought to want anyone's. But Hester's he wanted most fiercely.

Twice, he'd caught himself at the window of the study, just watching her move about, wisps of copper floating about her cheeks as she spoke to Dobbins or talked to the pigs while throwing them slops.

She'd been informing the sow of Drew's various deficits. Apparently, he snored rather loudly.

But the real shock was not his snoring, but the sight of his reflection in the glass of the window. He had the same love-struck look as his father used to have while watching Drew's beautiful mother.

Rather terrifying.

Last night, after he'd coaxed Hester to take his cock in her mouth, something she did with more enthusiasm than he'd expected, Drew had laid beside her, studying every inch of her with the awe of a man who first sees the painting of a master artist. Every freckle that spilled along her stomach was accounted for as well as a thorough inspection of the exact shade of the soft down between her thighs. There was nothing so exquisite as Hester Black.

Oh, the sounds she'd made as he worshipped her.

He was starting to suspect that Joshua Black had not made the decision to give Drew the farm, or his wife, lightly, but with great thought.

Drew shifted in the saddle. If he didn't cease his musings, riding would become incredibly uncomfortable for a sensitive part of his anatomy.

He started whistling again, so immersed in his thoughts of Hester that the sound of a pistol being fired, and the resulting thud of the bullet as it pierced the tree over his shoulder, didn't register immediately. Tugging on the reins, Drew looked around, half expecting to see a hunter come rushing out of the woods to apologize for being so careless.

He'd forgotten that the countryside could be as dangerous as London.

The second shot, whistling so close he felt the whoosh of air along his ear, spooked Drew's horse, nearly tossing him to the ground. Struggling to get control of the animal, he urged his horse forward in the direction of Blackbird Heath.

The third shot was far more accurate than the others.

A stinging sensation struck his thigh followed by a sharp bolt of pain along his thigh. Blood darkened the fabric of his trousers.

Steering his horse into the trees along the road, he deliberately wove in and out of the underbrush, hoping to make himself a difficult target, something Malcolm had once told him to do. A jealous husband or a sore loser at cards was bound to come after Drew sometime.

Or a disgruntled widow who wanted complete ownership of her home.

The thought was so ugly, so utterly devastating, Drew pushed it as far away as he could.

"Damn, that hurts." Blood was dripping down his leg into his boot and staining his trousers. He took out a handkerchief and pressed it against the wound, which was thankfully only a graze.

The thug in the alley who never demanded his purse. The strange intruder outside Blackbird Heath that night determined to bludgeon him. His initial suspicions, Drew dismissed, so *bloody busy tupping Hester* that he'd written off both incidents as common thievery or drunken mischief.

But being shot at, three times, was not coincidence. Not when there was only one person in all of Lincolnshire who could possibly benefit from Drew being dead.

And he was sharing a bed with her.

The pain of his gunshot wound matched that of his heart. Luckily, neither would kill him.

I'm a fool.

After a good stretch of time, Drew turned his horse back to the road, alert to anyone who could possibly be following him. But he was very close to Blackbird Heath. He doubted whoever shot at him would risk being seen by one of the farmhands.

Drew pressed a palm against his chest, willing the ache to stop. The horrible suspicion he'd harbored for weeks now screamed loudly in his head and he could no longer ignore it. He'd seen no signs of duplicity in Hester. No indication she was secretly planning his murder. If anything, she gave a noteworthy performance of a woman who was in love with him.

It can't be true. It can't.

He supposed it could be one of the other residents of Blackbird

Heath, all of whom would suffer if he sold the farm. But Drew thought Mrs. Ebersole far more likely to poison him than take shots. Dobbins was horribly nearsighted. Jake, well, there was a reason Hester only allowed him the simplest tasks. He was more likely to shoot himself than anyone else.

Drew rode back, relieved to see the house before him and stumbled as he dismounted. His thigh throbbed from the bullet; the entire length of his trousers now soaked in blood. The conclusion he'd arrived at was the only logical one. As unwelcome as it was.

A flash of red appeared at the corner of the house as the sun caught on the thick plait of Hester's hair, turning it to flame. "There you are. You're back from Horncastle sooner than I expected."

A smile of greeting graced her lovely mouth, which rarely pursed into an angry rosette any longer. She carried a basket of eggs over one arm, skirts fluttering about her ankles as she approached, looking innocent and lovely.

"Surprised to see me?" he said in a composed tone, careful to keep the sharp upper-crust accent in place purely because Drew knew Hester didn't care for it.

She halted at his tone, the slash of her brows drawing together. "Well, yes. I didn't expect you until closer to—" Hester's smile faltered as her eyes caught sight of the blood soaking his trousers. The basket of eggs dropped, several of them breaking or rolling about the grass.

"Drew, what happened?" Her hands reached for him.

"Don't touch me." Drew snapped. "Or pretend an ounce of concern."

"But you're hurt. What on earth happened? Let me—"

"Finish what you started?" He stepped out of her reach, barely able to look at her. As much as it—destroyed him, there simply wasn't anyone else. Only Hester would gain from his death. "My mother would have been impressed with your acting skills. You missed your calling."

"I've no idea what you're talking about, Drew. The loss of blood has made you nonsensical." She tried again to reach for him and he danced away.

"No, it was more the shots fired at me."

Hester's eyes widened. "Someone shot at you?" she said in disbelief. "Why on earth would anyone—"

"Just stop it. You must think me a complete fool. I'm not letting you anywhere near me, for all I know you've a blade strapped to your thigh or perhaps you've trained King George to peck me to death."

"Drew," she said carefully. "I don't know what you're talking about. Please let me see to your wound, you're bleeding everywhere. Maybe it was someone out hunting who didn't see you."

"Don't insult my intelligence a moment longer, Mrs. Black. I know it was you. You've long wanted to be rid of me. Well, you've failed once more."

Chapter Twenty-Three

Drew's words didn't sink in right away. She was too worried about the blood soaking through his trousers. The wound needed to be cleaned. It could become infected. She needed to summon a physician and—she blinked up at him. "I beg your pardon. You think I did this?"

"I underestimated you, Mrs. Black." Drew glared at her, hobbling up the steps to the front door. "I thought the worst you could do was put a snake in my bed." An ugly bark left him. "Or feed me cabbage. First a knife. Then nearly being bludgeoned. My only question is why it took you so long to use a pistol." Blood trailed behind him as he winced with each step.

"You were attacked in Horncastle?" Hester stuttered. "When?"

"As if you didn't know."

A cow had kicked her once in the stomach, this moment felt very much like that. She was shocked Drew would think she would ever hurt him. And he *did* believe it. She could see it in the chilling set to his handsome features and the frost in his tone. There was nothing but disdain for her in his eyes.

"I blame myself," he continued with a snarl. "I thought the thief in Horncastle only after my purse. The assailant outside my study window that night, well, your timely arrival and attempted seduction had me forgetting all about that particular incident, as I'm sure it was meant to." An ugly laugh came from him. "You tried to convince me I was foxed. Or met up with a random farmhand. One glimpse of your breasts with you nearly crawling into my lap had me forgetting all about it."

"That isn't what happened." Hester shot back, the warmth of the sun hit her skin which did nothing to banish the cold cruelty of Drew's words. Stubborn pride, the sort that had caused her a lifetime of misery reared its head. "You kissed *me*, as I recall," she bit out. "And I hadn't realized you'd find my worn, patched nightgown so incredibly seductive."

"Last night's performance was spectacular," he ground out. "One would never have thought you had ever taken a man's cock in your mouth before. Such innocent enthusiasm you displayed all the while planning my demise."

Hester took a step back, wavering as if she'd been slapped. Pummeled. Stomped upon. She inhaled sharply, smelling the dirt and chickens clinging to her skirts. A cloud above her head took away the light of the sun, or was that Drew's doing? An egg rolled beneath her foot, crunching as the shell shattered.

"You think that was a performance?"

She did not have a great deal of experience in physical relations. Or at least, she hadn't until meeting Drew. Hester had given herself over to Drew, trusting him completely. Allowing all sorts of intimate acts because she *loved* him. The words had not been said but—expressed by her in a variety of ways. Last night had been an act of intimacy for the man she loved, and he'd just crudely reduced it to nothing more than something any harlot could provide.

A sob tried to come up her throat, but she forced it down.

As horrible as it was to have Drew accuse her of wanting to commit murder, the knowledge he didn't really know her at all broke Hester.

"You can't even defend yourself." He shook his head. "I hadn't thought you so devious, Hester, but I should have guessed. You are willing to do anything for this bloody farm."

She was. This was proof that Blackbird Heath was the only thing she could ever depend on.

Lifting her chin, Hester refused to allow him to see how deeply he'd wounded her. "Tell me, how was I to accomplish this attempt on your life? Was I just lying in wait?"

"Oh, not you, per se. Someone in your employ," Drew said over his shoulder, as he limped up the steps to the house. "After all, you've had your chores to do. Can't miss gathering up the eggs just to have me murdered. Blackbird Heath must keep running smoothly."

Hester followed him up the steps and into the house. "You're dripping blood all over the floor. You'll ruin the rug."

He whipped around. "Go back to your bloody chickens and cows. Stop flinging dung about and hoping I'll step into it. You win, Hester. Blackbird Heath is yours. I'll be packed and out of here within the hour."

"You're leaving?" A deep hole opened up inside her.

"Didn't you hear me?" he hissed over his shoulder as he made his way slowly up the stairs to the room he hadn't slept in for weeks. "You win, Hester. Or are you following so that you can finish the job?"

Hester's jaw tightened. "Your wound. You can't even seat a horse."

"Maybe I'll bleed to death on the way to Horncastle." He stopped but did not look at her. "Tell me I'm wrong, Hester."

Hester stared back at him, ignoring the plea she heard in his words. If he was going to believe the worst of her, then so be it. Maybe this was just a way for Drew to rid himself of her. They'd never spoken of the future or if he'd ever return to London. He'd been looking for an excuse to leave her, she realized. Murder was as good as any.

"I refuse to dignify your accusations," she finally said, wrapping her pride and pain around her like a blanket.

"I thought as much. As I said, you've won this wager. I hate the bloody country and everything in it," he said pointedly.

Which included Hester.

"Go to London then." She flicked her hand dismissively. "Leave the countryside you so despise. You were only looking for a chance to leave." A terrible shattering occurred around her heart. "I find you to be overly dramatic. You must have learned how to act from your mother."

The mention of his mother caused such a torrent of emotions across Drew's handsome features, Hester almost took the words back.

He pointed to his bleeding thigh. "I tend to become overly dramatic when being shot at by a woman that—I've been bedding," he finished. "You could have just stabbed me in my sleep. I'm not sure why you didn't."

"I'd have to feed your body to the pigs," Hester snapped without thinking. "And I'd never get the blood out of the sheets."

His nostrils flared, jaw tilted in disdain. "Blackbird Heath is yours, Mrs. Black. It's the only thing…" he hesitated. "That matters to you at any rate."

She pressed her lips tightly together, unwilling to say anything more.

Let him go, her broken heart whispered.

Hester had given herself completely to Drew. Everything she possessed inside her. Told him things she had never told another. And it didn't matter. She would still be alone. Lifting her chin, she glared back at him.

"Nothing to add, Mrs. Black? No denials? I thought not."

"I believe nothing more needs to be said," she hurled at him, anger once more getting the best of her. Hester spun on her heel and left him to pack.

CHAPTER TWENTY-FOUR

HESTER SAT IN the parlor, hardening herself to the sight of the plain, black carriage Drew Sinclair had arrived in months ago now taking him away from Blackbird Heath. At least he hadn't attempted to ride to Horncastle. Mrs. Ebersole had been summoned, along with salve and bandages. Dobbins instructed to help with Drew's trunks.

If either was shocked by Drew's abrupt departure, they didn't show it.

She'd come back down the stairs and asked Mrs. Ebersole for tea, though Hester hadn't touched the steaming pot or the biscuits on a small plate beside it. This was for the best. Really. Drew had likely been the victim of a careless hunter, not anything nefarious. He was stringing together an unrelated series of coincidences in order to form a good excuse to leave her. It was the only explanation Hester could arrive at because *she* hadn't shot at him.

Hester had spent a great deal of her life alone. Solitary. Drew was no more than a pleasant interruption. This was always destined to be the only outcome of their relationship. He'd grown weary of the country, the animals, the crops. And especially Hester. He belonged in London, along with Mr. Worthington and Lady Downing.

Hester pressed a palm to her mid-section, feeling the catch of the callouses on her thumb against the muslin of her dress. She could never compete for his affections against the likes of that gorgeous creature.

She had not looked up when Drew came down the stairs, nor turned when he paused at the entrance of the parlor. A deep, drawn-out sigh had left him, his gaze burning the back of her neck, but he didn't speak. What more was there to say?

Once the carriage rolled out of sight, Hester rose and poured herself a brandy, ignoring the tea which had long since cooled. Belatedly, she considered that this might have been what made her father a sot. Losing the one thing he'd loved. Her mother.

Hester threw back the brandy, welcoming the sting as it traveled down her throat.

Father had become Horncastle's resident drunkard after Mother died, but Hester thought Thomas Morton had been headed down that path long before his wife fell ill. Certainly, he showed no talent for farming the land left to him by his father. The gambling and constant inebriation started as the farm began to fail. Poverty followed. She'd wed Joshua to escape her father, only to find herself in the orbit of yet another man who cared more for cards and dice than her.

But at least she'd had Blackbird Heath.

Hester pushed aside the past. It wasn't worth revisiting.

The more pressing concern, now that her emotions had calmed, was Drew's belief that Hester had tried to have him killed. Granted, she *had* tried to scare him off initially with the little garden snake and artfully placed clumps of dung, but those things were hardly murderous.

She thought back to the night she'd found Drew outside the study, clutching the wall, bloodied. He *did* look as if he were in his cups and merely stumbling about in the dark. If there was someone outside, Hester assumed it was a farmhand, perhaps a recently hired one, just roaming about. The last time Blackbird Heath had an intruder it was a man who tried to steal a chicken because he was hungry. Pastor was his name and he now managed Hester's sheep. Hardly deadly.

No one, to Hester's knowledge, had *ever* been stabbed for their purse in Horncastle, but admittedly, she didn't engage in gossip or travel into town often. The road where Drew claimed to have been shot was well-traveled, but hunting accidents did occur.

Taken all together, the events could be considered sinister in nature. If Drew were convinced someone was trying to get rid of him, given Hester's previous actions, it would be logical to assume she was the culprit.

"Except I love him," she whispered to the empty parlor. "How can he not feel the truth of that?"

But no one else had anything to gain except Hester if Drew relinquished his claim on Blackbird Heath either willingly, or because he was dead. Certainly, Martin Godwick didn't like the idea of Drew being here, and he'd been protective of Hester since Joshua's death, but that was hardly grounds for murder.

A hint of uneasiness slid through her recalling the conversation in Martin's office the day he'd attempted to kiss her. She'd put it down to his worry over Ellie. But could Martin—

Don't be ridiculous.

Hester was unlikely to inspire any gentleman with such passion. Not even Drew.

The thought had a choked sound come up her throat, no matter how she tried to stop it. In response, Hester poured another brandy.

If not Martin, could the culprit have been Mrs. Ebersole? Blackbird Heath was her home as much as Hester's. The housekeeper had been in place long before Joshua and Hester wed. She knew a great many people in Horncastle, there must be at least a few who would have been willing to accept Mrs. Ebersole's coin in return for scaring away Drew.

More ridiculous.

Dobbins? Jake? Hester thought it unlikely.

If indeed someone was trying to harm Drew, it was far more apt to be someone from his past life. He'd made his living at cards. Seduced a great many women. There had to be at least a handful of jealous husbands wanting to take their revenge on Drew. Or a fellow gambler who didn't take kindly to losing his purse. Either of those options were better candidates for murdering him than Hester. Yet he'd jumped to the conclusion that it was her, or someone she'd hired. As if she could spare the coin. Drew had seen the ledgers for Blackbird Heath.

But his accusations did give him the excuse to return to London.

The hum of pain pressed over her heart once more.

What was worse? To have him think her capable of murder or merely using it as a way to rid himself of Hester. She supposed it didn't matter. He was gone.

Hester stared out the window facing the curved drive of Blackbird Heath for hours, hoping Drew would come to his senses and return. Long ago, when this had been more stately manor than farm, the lord and lady of the house had probably awaited the arrival of guests in much the same manner, with a warm fire and a glass of brandy at their elbow.

But as the shadows lengthened across the fields surrounding Blackbird Heath, there was no sign of the sleek conveyance that had first brought a gentleman from London to her door.

Andrew Sinclair was not returning to Blackbird Heath.

Or Hester.

Chapter Twenty-Five

Hester stretched her aching neck until a satisfying pop sounded. She'd been helping in the fields, bringing in the sugar beets though Blackbird Heath had more than enough hired hands to help. Yesterday, she'd ridden up across the slope where the sheep grazed, searching for a lamb that went missing. She worked each day, from King George's first crow until twilight swept across the long grass, attempting to heal her broken heart or at least, stop the bleeding. Over a fortnight had passed since Drew stormed out and Hester had given up hope he would ever return.

And she didn't care. In the least.

There had only been one small fit of weeping which Hester put down to the sugar beet harvest being smaller than she'd hoped.

Turning the corner, she strode towards the house, stomach grumbling and hoping Mrs. Ebersole wouldn't be opposed to serving dinner early. A horse stood tied just outside the house, stomping its feet. Hester's entire chest leapt in excitement. She quickened her pace but soon halted. The horse was one she recognized as belonging to Martin Godwick.

The first week of Drew's departure, Hester had spent in a stew of frustration, anger, and longing. She didn't want to accept that his leaving was due to lack of affection for her. You'd think a rake of Drew's experience wouldn't resort to using attempted murder as an excuse to break things off but use something with a bit more finesse.

Also, there was the matter that Drew had been shot in the thigh.

A hunting accident. It had to be. The other incidents were mere coincidences.

Hester supposed she would receive word from Drew eventually, or at least his solicitor. She rolled all her feelings for him into a tiny ball, a small nugget that she only examined very late at night when her bed seemed far too large for one person.

But the emptiness inside Hester persisted. There was no pride in the harvest. No satisfaction at the honey production of her bees. Only exhaustion which never ceased. Melancholy. The cows were just cows. The sheep nothing special. Hester wasn't accustomed to missing someone.

Sighing, she gave Martin's horse a gentle pat on his nose before going up the steps into the house. Hester forced a polite smile on her lips and walked into the parlor. Oddly enough, she'd given Martin or Joshua's will little thought since Drew's departure, but seeing him sitting so casually in her parlor, had the skin prickling on the back of her neck. Unease took root inside her at the sight of her solicitor.

And Hester couldn't put her finger on why, exactly.

"Hester," Martin rose as she entered the room. A glass filled with amber liquid sat at his elbow though it wasn't even noon. "I hope you don't mind that I helped myself. Now that Sinclair is gone, I decided to celebrate. I found a bottle of Irish whiskey. I'll assume he left it behind."

How would Martin know Drew preferred Irish whiskey? Or that Drew was gone? "How did you know he'd returned to London?"

"Sinclair told me himself." He tossed a small packet on the table. "Stopped by my offices on his way to London and informed me to expect correspondence from his solicitor. Which arrived late yesterday."

So, Drew was back in London. As expected. "What is it?" She nodded to the packet.

"The deed to Blackbird Heath, which is now yours. Sinclair signed over the estate to you and the deed has been duly filed in London *and* Horncastle. Congratulations." He lifted his glass, took a swallow and grimaced. "Awful stuff. Brandy is what I prefer."

"Sinclair came to your offices?" Hester asked, attempting to keep her voice from trembling even though inside, the last flicker of hope inside her died. Drew really wasn't coming back.

"I'll admit, when Sinclair stopped by my offices, I was shocked. But after informing me how tedious he found the country and the drabness of life at Blackbird Heath; Sinclair expressed his desire to be rid of the estate and return it to you. He was vastly amused at your desire to be his land manager."

"Was he?"

"He confessed that he allowed you to think the idea under consideration because it amused him." Martin shrugged. "Jaded rogue. Always seeking out new ways to entertain himself."

Hester swayed, ever so slightly.

"I'm sorry to tell you this, Hester. I probably shouldn't." Martin glanced at her from beneath his lashes. "But Sinclair, after we shared a brandy, admitted to a wager he'd made with one of his friends from London. Apparently, this friend didn't believe Sinclair could survive more than a week in the countryside. A large purse was at stake." Martin shook his head. "Ever the gambler. I assume he'd wager on anything."

She forced herself into one of the chairs. "I'm not sure what to say."

"I can't imagine he'd ever return to Lincolnshire. I'm only relieved that he agreed Blackbird Heath rightfully belonged to you."

"Most—welcome news."

"I think so. I had nearly exhausted my efforts to force his departure," Martin smiled.

Hester gripped the arms of the chair. "Forced?"

"With Bishop Franks, of course," he assured her with a wink. "Unfortunately, the rumors of your relationship with Sinclair were making things difficult with the good bishop." Martin nodded to the papers sitting on the table between them. "But thankfully, there's no need to do *anything* else." He shook his head. "Though I would have gladly done more. The official document from Sinclair's solicitor. A man named—"

"Patchahoo," Hester finished. Wager? She refused that to be the case. Drew didn't even *know* Martin Godwick. She found it highly unlikely he would share a brandy and confess that his relationship with Hester was no more than a wager made to him by a friend.

"I never understood why Sinclair was so determined to sell Blackbird Heath. He doesn't need the money. Cuts quite a swathe through London by lifting every skirt he meets and fleecing their husbands of cards." A tiny grin lifted Martin's lips. A cruel one.

"He's a gambler," Hester offered. "Such men always need a steady source of funds."

"Yes, but Andrew Sinclair is *also* the brother of the Earl of Emerson."

"The Earl of Emerson?" Hester regarded Martin carefully. Drew had mentioned his brother and all his siblings with great affection, but he'd left out the fact his brother was an earl.

"I found out quite accidentally," Martin continued. "From an acquaintance lately returned from London. Sinclair is one of the finest rakes in London society, I'm told."

Yes, and Martin seemed delighted to remind Hester of that fact, repeatedly.

"Runs in a fast set," he continued. "One of his closest friends is the younger brother of Viscount Worthington."

Her heart thudded. "Mr. Worthington attended the house party."

"Well, there you have it." Martin snapped his fingers. "What sort of gentleman must you be to find amusement by toying with some poor widow in the country? Threatening to sell your home and demanding to live here must have been vastly entertaining. Not to mention parading you about when his friends arrived from London while laughing behind your back. How *cruel*."

The corner of Martin's left eye twitched in an alarming manner.

"After all, the brother of an earl has little use for you or Blackbird Heath."

Hester's heart thudded dully in her ears, panic rose deep inside that she was unable to push away. Had she truly been so gullible? Martin made sense, in a terrible, horrible way.

"But I'm sure he enjoyed your attempts to convince him to allow you to manage the estate for him." Martin leaned closer and Hester had to stop herself from flinching. "*Did* he enjoy your attempts, Hester?" His fingers stretched and released along his thigh, then began to beat out a rhythm. Like a deranged drummer.

"I don't believe that is any of your affair, Martin." A wave of dizziness assailed her. "Nor is it true."

"Oh, I think it is. I've spent a good amount of time listening to the conjecture about you and Sinclair in Horncastle. So much ugly gossip in Horncastle. I was forced to defend you, Hester. I could have allowed you to flounder but did not."

A trickle of fear slid down her spine. This entire conversation had grown inappropriate and Martin's behavior far too unsettling for Hester. She listened for Mrs. Ebersole, or even Mary in the hall, but the house was silent.

"I never asked you to defend me, Martin."

"There are many things you never asked of me, yet I did them all the same. You could at least show me some appreciation for my efforts." His palm slapped on the arm of the chair he sat in.

Hester jumped at the sound. "What exactly have you done, Martin?" She was almost afraid to hear the answer because it would make her a fool *many* times over. Drew *had* been shot; she'd seen the blood darkening the fabric of his trousers. That fact was irrefutable. But she no longer assumed it to be an accident.

Martin regarded her with a slow burning intensity filling the blue of his eyes. "I thought you'd be happier. I'm rather disappointed that you are not."

"You don't look well, Martin." Hester tried to stay calm.

"I'm perfectly fine."

But he wasn't, his fingers kept jerking about and the twitch of his left eye was unnatural. And why was the house so bloody quiet? Why hadn't Mary at least come in to offer tea? "I—believe I'll find Mrs. Ebersole." She stood. "Some tea might set you to rights." Her skin prickled with the urgency to get away from Martin. "Maybe some of those little cakes. You like those, don't you?"

"Mrs. Ebersole isn't here. Sit." Martin pointed back to the chair Hester had just vacated. "Nor Mary, if that is your next thought. Mary's sister was involved in an accident with a cart just outside Horncastle. Nearly crushed beneath the wheels. Dobbins must have rushed off to lend help as well, as I didn't see him about. A terrible tragedy for all concerned." He blinked rapidly, wiping at his twitching eye with one hand.

Panic hummed along Hester's arms.

"I thought we needed some privacy, and all your farmhands are so bloody helpful." A hard, manic light shone from him, much like the one she'd briefly glimpsed in his office that day in Horncastle. "I expect Mary's sister has at worst, a broken leg. She won't be lame." He tapped his chin. "At least I don't think so."

"I should join them," she said.

Hindsight was often crystal clear. You wondered at all the signs that were right before you but refused to see. Madness, for one. Martin's state of mind showed in every tic of his body. How had she never noticed?

He's planned all of this.

"I don't think so, Hester." He gave her a patient look, left eye still jerking madly. "I love you to the point of distraction, Hester. Truly. But at times, Hester, I have to wonder at your stubborn stupidity. Blackbird Heath is a perfect example." He wiggled a finger at her.

The use of her name, repeatedly, had her feeling as if she were nothing more than a dog Martin was trying to train. Or she was being chastised like an unruly child. "You are my solicitor. I don't think you should address me in such a manner."

"No wife of mine," he continued, ignoring her completely. "Will be working like a common farmhand every day. I really can't allow it." Several beats passed. "Hester."

Her throat tightened every time he said her name. Obviously, something was not right with her solicitor. "I'm—not marrying you." The very idea was loathsome, given Martin had likely been the person behind the attempts on Drew's life. And she thought he might be mad.

And Drew? He hadn't been looking for an excuse to be rid of Hester. He honestly believed she had been trying to kill him.

"Darling Hester, yes, you are." He gave her an adoring look. "I've proven myself worthy of you. I've gone to great lengths so that we can be together. And if you defy me after we're wed," the crazed look in his eyes returned. "I'll be forced to sell Blackbird Heath. I won't tolerate your disobedience, Hester." Martin reached over and chucked her beneath the chin. "I simply won't."

She felt as if she were suffocating. "You shot at him. It was you."

"I bungled that entire situation. Couldn't get a clear shot. I lost my temper. But considering Sinclair's brother is an earl, I'm glad I missed. But fate is on our side, Hester. Now we can be together. *Finally.* Sinclair was mucking things up."

Martin didn't want Blackbird Heath.

He wants me.

The air whooshed out of her lungs and Hester fell back in her chair, stunned by the depth of Martin's madness. He'd been part of her existence for years, first as the son of her husband's solicitor and then her friend. Never once had he given any indication that he harbored such feelings for her.

"I should like you to leave, Mr. Godwick." Hester tried to put some distance between them, though given the circumstances she thought it unlikely to work. "Please. I think you—have been overwhelmed by Ellie's death. I won't turn you in to the constable. I promise. But you must seek the help of a physician. You aren't well."

Martin's nostrils flared, eyes wild. "I'm better than I have ever been. If you don't. Stop. Being. So. Difficult." Each word fell on her like a slap. "You will force me to compel you to do so. *Hester*. Take Mrs. Ebersole, for instance. Sour woman. Face like a rotted mushroom. The world won't miss her. Is that what you want, *Hester*?"

Her entire body jolted each time he said her name.

"Is it, Hester? Do you need me to show you what will happen if you continue to be coy?"

Coy? She was terrified. "Please," Hester whispered. "Please don't harm Mrs. Ebersole." Fear and panic bubbled up her throat was so thick; she was sure to choke on it. He knew how much she loved Blackbird Heath and the people that resided here. They were her family. Her eyes darted about searching for anything she could use as a weapon, but nothing was in reach.

"I don't," he ran his hand through the short waves of his hair, pulling at the ends. "Understand why you are so reluctant. You have been encouraging my affection for years, Hester, and now you've caught it."

Dear God.

Her mind raced over every interaction with Martin, each sentence or look. The most she'd done was take his arm at Joshua's funeral.

"Do you want everyone at Blackbird Heath to be struck by a terrible stomach ailment?" he giggled, the sound echoing unpleasantly over Hester's arms. "The same ailment that killed my poor…" his features grew mournful. "Ellie."

"What—" Horror filled her at the implication of his words. She might be ill. "You killed Ellie."

"Well, how else could we be together? She was in the way." He rolled his eyes. "Oh, don't look at me like that, Hester. You snap the necks of your chickens all the time. I merely put some glass in her food. Just a little here and there. Mainly in the tiny cakes she insisted upon having with her tea. You practically begged me to do so, pretending so much shyness when I confessed my feelings."

Hester sobbed, holding on to the chair as she stood. Martin had murdered his wife. "You need help. Your mind is distressed. I'll just summon the physician, shall I?"

"Stop saying that." He moved quicker than Hester expected, fingers circling around her wrist. He bent her hand back and forth while Hester struggled to get away from him.

"You use your right hand to compose letters, do you not?"

Hester nodded mutely.

"Good. I don't want to be surprised. Sinclair is left-handed. I won't make that mistake again. Now," Martin's eyes filled with concern. "I won't break your right wrist, *but*—" he took her other hand. "I might snap your left if you don't do as you're told. I understand a broken wrist is painful." Another crazed bit of laughter bubbled out of him. "Now, come here." Pulling Hester to the corner of the room, he pushed her towards the small desk in the corner.

Hester's pulse thumped painfully. She was more afraid than she'd ever been in her life.

"You do have some writing paper in there, don't you?" He nodded at the desk. "Sinclair has taken over your study, so I assume you tend to your correspondence here instead. Did you actually give him permission to go through your account books?"

"It was *you* outside the study that night." Martin had been sneaking about Blackwood Heath. Spying on them.

"You act as if I don't get my hands dirty." Another roll of his eyes. "Honestly, Hester. Of course, it was me. But I wasn't trying to kill him, necessarily, only hoping to knock him unconscious. I would have poured brandy all over him and made it look as if he'd run into the wall. A well placed blow to the head and a person can bleed to death. That's what happened to my father."

Hester gripped the edge of the desk to keep from toppling over. Martin's father had died from a fall down the stairs. He'd hit his head and—

Oh, Dear god.

"I did adore the sight of you running out to him like an angel of mercy." His breath fanned her cheek. "I could see right through your nightgown."

Hand shaking, Hester opened the desk and took out a piece of paper, discreetly sliding a letter opener into her sleeve. Her mouth went dry as she picked up a pen. Martin had likely murdered his father. He'd killed his wife. There was no telling what he would do to Mrs. Ebersole or poor Mary.

"Put the letter opener back, darling Hester. Do you think I'm an idiot?" He grabbed her wrist and shook the letter opener free. "I might use this to stab the first person I come across. Or one of your beloved cows."

"No, Martin." A vision of Tabby, bloodied and dead in the barn, flashed before her. "I'm—sorry. It is just that you're frightening me."

He pressed a kiss to the top of her head and Hester struggled not to push him away in disgust. "I know I can be excitable at times. I apologize. Now, you will write exactly what I tell you, Hester darling."

Her skin chilled at the endearment.

"The first time I saw the sunlight strike your hair," he murmured, "Was akin to watching a flame come to life. I knew then you were meant to be mine, Hester darling." His voice hardened. "I didn't want to marry Ellie, you know. My father forced me into it."

Martin Godwick, wealthy, handsome, and brilliant was once the most sought-after bachelors in Horncastle. He was a highly respected solicitor, as his father had been. Considered to be one of the most morally upstanding gentlemen in all of Lincolnshire.

And he was a *murderer*.

How had no one seen the madness lurking behind the cool blue of his eyes?

Martin cleared his throat and began to dictate:

"Mrs. Ebersole,

I've found that I need a respite from my duties to Blackbird Heath. The last few years, beginning with the death of my beloved husband, have left me with a desire to collect my thoughts in private. I've gone to Lincoln to enjoy myself for a few days. Do not be alarmed at my absence. You may reach me at the Obergon Hotel. I'll return at the end of the week."

The note was vague even with the mention of a hotel which Hester was certain didn't exist. Mrs. Ebersole would *never* assume Hester would go off on her own to visit Lincoln on some sort of holiday. Not with half the sugar beets still in the field. Or all of Hester's things upstairs. But Hester mentioned none of that to Martin. He'd already hurt Mary's sister for no other reason than to clear the house so he could—

Hester looked at the note she'd just written, dread sinking into her bones.

Martin was taking her somewhere.

"Off we go." He pulled her up by the elbow and took her arm as if they were about to promenade. "My horse is outside."

She went with him, numb but with the hope that Mrs. Ebersole would realize that the letter was a pretext. Or perhaps Dobbins would. If Drew were here, he would see the lies written in her hand.

Yes, but he isn't here.

"My pistol is loaded and in my pocket. I don't expect we'll see anyone, but if we do, I'll shoot them if you do more than smile. Understand, darling Hester?" He lifted her into the saddle and then climbed up behind her.

"Where are we going?"

"Somewhere you'll be safe. I've got to secure a marriage license and I certainly can't do so in Grantham or Horncastle, can I? Society is unlikely to be understanding of our quick marriage so soon after Ellie's death. I considered just running off to Scotland, but I've no desire to be married over an anvil or give any reason to invalidate our marriage." He made a disdainful sound. "I am a prominent member of Horncastle. I have a reputation to protect. But I've found someone who is willing to assist me in securing a license, so don't you worry, darling. Our vows will be ironclad."

Hester cringed as Martin wrapped his arm around her waist. She hadn't thought he'd take her to Horncastle, but she had hoped that a more populated town or city would give her the chance to slip away.

"I'll visit Blackbird Heath in a day or so and pretend great surprise that you've gone to Lincoln by yourself. As a gentleman, and your solicitor, I will volunteer to go to Lincoln and find you." His hold on her tightened. "We'll be wed and return to Blackbird Heath. A whirlwind romance."

Hester stared straight ahead, her stubborn resolve hardening to stone inside her.

She *would* get away from Martin.

Somehow.

Chapter Twenty-Six

"Drew." Jordan clapped him on the back, holding out a glass of whisky. "I've insulted you at least a half-dozen times since you entered the drawing room. Sniveling popinjay."

"Scurrilous fop." Tamsin sidled over.

"Ratbag," Aurora whispered to him.

"Stop," Drew laughed. "I am merely preoccupied, somewhat. And I did not expect to be welcomed to Tamsin's wedding by being slandered." He pinched the bridge of his nose. "Dear God, that sounds so strange. Tamsin and wedding in the same sentence."

Tamsin raised a brow. "I'm to be a duchess. You'll have to call me 'Your Grace.'"

Drew snorted. "Never. No duchess I've ever met goes about breaking noses and punching gentlemen in their stomachs."

"She doesn't do that anymore." A massive presence loomed over Drew's sister, blocking the sunlight coming through the drawing room window. "At least not that I'm aware of."

The Duke of Ware, one of the largest and certainly the most eccentric dukes in England gazed at Tamsin with rapt adoration, discreetly ogling her bosom. His massive arm lingered along the delicate curve of her back with sharp possessiveness. Not that anyone would ever challenge Ware for Tamsin. Drew's sister was an acquired taste for most, though she was stunningly beautiful. Far too bold. Opinionated. Preferred breeches to petticoats. And possessed a right hook that would take your chin off.

Drew wished Ware all the best.

They were gathered in the drawing room at Emerson House and shortly to be seated in the dining room, to celebrate the upcoming nuptials of the scandalous Tamsin Sinclair to His Grace, the Duke of Ware. Honestly, he'd been terribly confused when he arrived in London. Drew had assumed the reason for the ridiculous charade the two were involved in at the end of the last Season had been to avoid this *very thing*.

"I'm pleased you managed to make time to return to London. Did you sell the estate or was it a farm?" Jordan asked. "Patchahoo wasn't very clear."

Patchahoo, who had the hearing of a hunting dog, raised his chin and stopped his discussion with Jordan's wife Odessa, to say, "I was abundantly clear, my lord. It is an estate that has become a farm. I'm not sure why you find the information to be confusing."

Jordan turned back to Drew. "Well, that doesn't muddy the waters at all. If Patchahoo wasn't so bloody good at soliciting and managing the affairs of Dunnings, I'd show him the door." His brother said the last to ensure the solicitor didn't miss his remarks.

"I take it the coal mining operation is going well." Drew sipped his whiskey. He'd missed good Irish whiskey.

"It is. To be clear, if you want to spend the rest of your life doing nothing more than playing cards, I'm assured by Patchahoo that you can."

Drew smiled back and lifted his glass, knowing now that he had only to ask for the sum he needed to form the partnership with Worth and Jordan would give it to him. It wouldn't even be charity. Patchahoo, on Jordan's instructions, had set up a trust for each of his siblings. None of the Sinclairs need ever worry over money or banishment ever again.

"I've other plans," Drew answered, not ready to mention the partnership with Worth.

"So," Jordan regarded him over the edge of his own whiskey. "Did you sell the estate in Lincolnshire? You were there overly long, which I found out of character given you detest the country."

"I don't detest it. I—found I enjoyed myself." Drew had belatedly realized, after stepping back into Emerson House, that London no longer held his attention as it once had. The streets were too crowded and noisy. The amusements seemed frivolous. Not even an evening with Worth had improved his mood.

"Who is she?" Jordan was watching him, lips tilted in a grin.

Home.

Home for Drew wasn't a place, but a person. And it came in the form of a stubborn, shrewish red-headed widow. Only he hadn't known it until now.

An entire fortnight had gone by and with each passing day, the ache over leaving Hester had intensified until it now bloomed over Drew's chest with a stinging awareness that could no longer be ignored. He was happy to see his family. Thrilled for Tamsin, though he did worry for Ware's safety. But over the course of the afternoon and into this evening, the ache had morphed into a sensation of impending doom, an insidious creeping dread that Drew couldn't ignore no matter the merriment surrounding him.

He blamed Hester's annoying solicitor, Godwick.

The solicitor reminded Drew quite a bit of King George in his strutting about, although he found Godwick far less useful than the rooster. He didn't bother to hide his pleasure at Drew's announcement that he was giving Blackbird Heath to Hester and leaving Lincolnshire.

Glee, not pleasure. Godwick was *gleeful*. An emotion one usually associated with a young girl, for instance. So strange to see it on the face of a well-respected solicitor. Especially one who had recently lost his wife to a mysterious ailment. There was also the possessive way Godwick spoke of Hester while assuring Drew he would file the papers for Blackbird Heath on her behalf.

And, he'd called her Hester. *Not* Mrs. Black.

The strangeness of that conversation gnawed away at Drew the second he strode out of Godwick's office. At the time, Drew had still been furious at Hester. She hadn't even denied trying to murder him.

Drew frowned.

Well, she hadn't denied it enough.

Now, looking back at the conversation with Martin Godwick, the solicitor's obvious affection for Hester far exceeded mere friendship.

Once he'd returned to London Drew found he could no longer sleep past dawn—something he might never forgive King George for—which left him a great deal of time to review a handful of pertinent facts.

If Hester had truly wanted Drew dead, she would have come up with a foolproof means of ending his life. She was not a woman who lacked determination or intelligence. The grass snake she'd put in his bed *could* have been an adder had she wished it to be. Hiring a trio of assailants didn't strike Drew as something Hester would waste her coin on. Poison was easier and less costly. Mrs. Ebersole could have served him toadstools in a butter sauce with some fish and Drew would have dropped dead before figuring out he'd been murdered.

She wore her emotions on her face, blushing at the slightest innuendo. Which meant Hester was unlikely to pretend affection or passion. Her skin flushed with arousal for Drew at every turn.

A vision of Hester, sleeping next to him, her small, reddened workworn palm placed firmly over his heart flashed before him.

I'm such a bloody idiot.

"There you go again, Drew." Jordan took his arm and pulled him away from the others. "What happened in Lincolnshire that you are so determined to stay there?"

"How did you know, Jordan." Drew lifted his glass in the direction of his brother's wife, a slip of a thing with honey brown hair. "That it should be Odessa?"

"I didn't. Not at first. But even when she was parading about looking like a troll, I felt a pull in her direction. She's clever and odd. Funny. Devoted," Jordan murmured, love shining from his eyes as he watched Odessa laugh at something Patchahoo said. "And," he shrugged. "She made her case to me while riding through the park in a closed carriage."

Hester was clever. Brave. Determined. Passionate. Horribly stubborn and full of pride. Her anger towards him wasn't denial, but because of Drew's accusations. And he'd been too stubborn himself to see it.

He missed Hester desperately. So much so, Drew didn't want to spend another second away from her. "I need to leave for Horncastle at once. There is something I need to do there, something I've neglected. I know it's late. I know—"

"Go." Jordan plucked the glass of whiskey from Drew's fingers with a knowing look. "Try to get everything resolved before the wedding. Tamsin will want you here." He nodded in the direction of their sister who was dangling from Ware's arm. "I'll make your excuses."

DREW TRAVELED THROUGH the night, carrying only a small valise with a change of clothes. The sense of urgency over Hester had grown into full blown panic, since he'd unceremoniously slipped from Emerson House. When finally, travel-weary and covered in dust, he rode up to the door of Blackbird Heath, Drew knew the second his feet touched the ground that Hester wasn't here. The entire farm seemed to ache from her absence.

Leaping up the steps, he raised his hand to knock, realized how stupid that was, and reached for the knob only to have the door wrenched open. Mrs. Ebersole, dour and in an ill humor as usual, greeted him, but there was also profound relief in her craggy features as she saw him.

"Mr. Sinclair."

"Where is she?" he asked, walking into the house. Mud fell from his boots and dust from his coat. The unease inside him grew stronger.

The housekeeper trailed him. "She's gone. I'm—nearly two days ago, Mrs. Black left a note in the parlor. Said she was going to Lincoln on holiday."

"Lincoln?" Drew stopped at the base of the stairs. "Why would she go to Lincoln?" The rising panic increased to a torrent. "Mrs. Black went on holiday," he said in disbelief. "While the sugar beets were being harvested? And the bloody cabbages?"

"I wasn't here, Mr. Sinclair." Mrs. Ebersole took a step back. "Mary's sister had an accident. Nearly crushed by a cart outside of Horncastle. I—well, Mrs. Black was with her bees at the time, and I didn't want to bother her. I expected to return shortly, well before supper. I went to help. Poor girl was sorely injured. We don't know how—"

"Mrs. Ebersole, I'm truly sorry for Mary's sister. But where is Mrs. Black?"

"I don't know," she choked out. "We returned to Blackbird Heath late and I didn't even see Mrs. Black's note or realize she was gone until the following morning, when Dobbins came looking for her. I checked her room, but all her things are still there. She didn't take a horse or anything else. Did she go to Lincoln in her work clothes and boots? Why wouldn't she take that lovely olive gown?" She bit her lip. "Mrs. Black has never been further than Horncastle her whole life, Mr. Sinclair. She would never venture to Lincoln on her own. Nor abandon the farm for so long."

"Agreed, Mrs. Ebersole."

"And Mr. Godwick—"

"What about Godwick?" Drew felt the fear sink deep into his bones at the mention of the solicitor.

Mrs. Ebersole paused, wringing her hands. "Well, Mr. Godwick stopped in yesterday, looking for Mrs. Black. He was...*twitchy.*"

"Twitchy?"

"Like a dog that has fleas. Jerking about. Acting odd. He asked to see Mrs. Black. When I informed him she'd gone to Lincoln, he didn't act surprised that Mrs. Black was gone."

Drew would bet his purse that Hester wasn't in Lincoln. Or Horncastle. Godwick had somehow coaxed her to write that note, because Drew knew Hester would never willingly leave Blackbird Heath. The entire trip to Lincolnshire, he'd examined over and over what he knew of the solicitor, starting with the obvious delay in informing Drew of Blackbird Heath. His acquaintance with Godwick was brief, but Drew could sense a *wrongness* about him.

"Mr. Godwick offered to go to Lincoln and check on Mrs. Black for me," the housekeeper continued. "Said maybe she'd run off with an amorous suitor and would return a married woman. Then he winked at me." Mrs. Ebersole looked up at Drew, worry shining in her homely features. "But you're her," she cleared her throat and waved about a hand. "Suitor."

Godwick wanted to be that suitor. The solicitor had much to gain from Drew's leaving Lincolnshire. No wonder he'd been so bloody happy. The attempts on Drew's life had never been about Blackbird Heath.

"He's taken her," he said with certainty to Mrs. Ebersole, knowing he was right. "Godwick."

"But—" A palm flew up to cover her lips. "Why would Mr. Godwick lie to me? Why would he take her?"

"To make sure you or anyone else wouldn't go looking for Mrs. Black." He placed a hand on the housekeeper's shoulder. "I believe Godwick to be unstable. Mad, even. And the mad do things for no reason at all."

Chapter Twenty-Seven

Hester lay on her back, careful to keep her breathing deep and even so that Martin wouldn't suspect she was awake. He'd long since divested her of her clothes, stating the dress and apron smelled of animals and dirt. She still had her chemise, though it was little protection. At least Martin had the decency to cover her with a blanket.

Two days. That was how long it had been since Martin forced her on to his horse at Blackbird Heath. No one had seen them leave given he'd conveniently coordinated events so that Mrs. Ebersole and Mary were gone from the house. Hester had made the mistake of struggling, trying to fling herself off the saddle as they started down the road away from Blackbird Heath. Martin's fingers had closed around her throat until she had gasped for breath. The world had gone dark, and when Hester awoke, it was to find herself half-naked and tied to this bed. She was in a small cottage of some sort, one layered in dust from disuse. A rickety table and two chairs stood in one corner along with a collection of fishing poles.

And she'd been completely alone.

Hester had screamed, praying someone would hear her as the light outside the dirty windows began to dim. But no one came. Not even Martin.

Hester spent a sleepless night struggling against her bindings, cursing Martin, and wishing for all the world that Drew would suddenly appear. Impossible, of course. Andrew Sinclair had left believing that the woman who he'd shared a bed with was capable of murdering him over a bloody farm. Hester and her stubborn pride had done little to dissuade him.

When she awoke yesterday morning, it had been to stare at the ceiling above her, trying to decide if the water stain resembled a rabbit or a dog because it kept her from screaming again. Or weeping. Hester thought of Drew with the terrible knowledge that she would never see him again. He would never know it had been Martin, or that Hester loved him.

When Martin finally appeared, Hester was relieved if only because she'd been worried he meant to leave her to starve. He fed her some cheese and a bit of bread, informing her that she was in the fishing cabin once owned by Mason Godwick, his father.

Hester must have regarded him with some hope because Martin then went on to assure her that no one remembered Mason had enjoyed fishing or kept a small, well-hidden sanctuary in the woods. Best of all, no one was looking for her. Everyone at Blackbird Heath believed Hester was in Lincoln. He'd visited Mrs. Ebersole and assured her *he* would go to Lincoln and fetch Hester home.

That was part of Martin's grand scheme. Telling everyone that he'd gone to Lincoln to retrieve Hester where they would miraculously fall in love and return to Horncastle, married. It was a stupid plan but would likely work given no one but Mrs. Ebersole and Dobbins gave a fig for Hester. She didn't have any friends or family. Or anyone who might care at all.

Her heart squeezed inside her chest thinking of Drew. Would it matter to him if he ever returned to Lincolnshire and found her wed to this madman? Or was he already back out in society having forgotten all about Hester?

Martin had stayed a while longer, annoyed at Hester's efforts to ignore him and finally stormed off, leaving her alone for another night.

She didn't even bother to scream for help. No one would hear her.

"I know you aren't asleep, Hester," Martin drawled, stepping closer to loom over her. "You can't fool me."

Hester's eyes popped open, to glare at her captor. Freshly shaved. Clean clothes. Maniacal gleam in his pale blue eyes. Nothing had changed. She wanted to turn her head and ignore him, but her bladder felt as if it might burst.

"I must see to my needs, Martin." She jerked at the rope binding her wrists to the bed. "Privately."

The bed dipped with his weight as he sat beside her. His fingers stroked along her cheek and jaw. "Not alone, my darling Hester. I can't trust you not to run off."

She pulled from his touch. "Won't the good people of Horncastle find it strange that you must keep your bride tied up?"

Martin's left eye twitched.

"You have such a sharp tongue, my darling Hester." He untied all but a long length of rope attached to her ankle and knotted so tightly that Hester would need a knife to free herself. And if he called her 'his darling Hester' one more time, she may use the rope to strangle herself.

He led her outside to the privy, little more than a small wooden enclosure, some distance from the cabin. The outhouse was full of spiders and smelled terrible, but she would have some privacy.

Hester went inside and did her best to slam the door on Martin's smiling face. Impossible with the bloody rope in the way. Her entire body trembled, terrified at the thought that she wouldn't be able to free herself before Martin's plans came to fruition. He'd found someone to perform the marriage, someone who Hester suspected wasn't too concerned with the fact that the bride was being wed against her will nor that a special license had to be procured. A vicar, she supposed, from one of the smaller villages in the area who was in dire need of the coin. Martin had not given her the details.

The rope around her ankle jerked through the door.

"Hurry along, darling Hester. There are preparations to be made. I've got to fetch your dress." A sigh came from Martin through the door. "Blue silk. Stunning frock. You'll be an exquisite bride. Now don't berate me, darling Hester, for wanting a private ceremony. I want you all to myself."

Hester's fingers shook as she saw to her needs. "When will this ceremony take place?"

"Tomorrow," Martin said through the door. "I've several errands to attend to in addition to your lovely frock. You must have a ring of some sort, after all."

She flung open the door, one of the warped boards coming loose. "I'm not marrying you. I'll scream during the entire ceremony. I doubt any vicar you've found will agree to wed a hysterical bride."

"Don't you dare embarrass me, Hester. Mrs. Ebersole's very existence depends upon it. She's older. More likely to trip and hit her head while going about her business. As my father did." Martin giggled.

Hester's fingers dug into the frayed wood of the door.

"Oh, don't frown so. I hate it when we argue." He gave her an adoring look, as if he'd merely told her an amusing story instead of admitting he'd killed Mason Godwick.

Hester inhaled a lungful of the chilly, morning air, trying to keep from giving into her fear and falling, weeping, to the ground. Martin would threaten and hold Blackbird Heath and everyone in it, over her head for an eternity. Her only hope was to escape him at some point.

Hester had felt hopeless many times in her life, most recently when Drew left her at Blackbird Heath. But deranged and dangerous Martin Godwick was more than even Hester was prepared for.

Her foot stumbled over a tree root and Martin caught her.

He escorted her back to the cabin, the rope in his hand as if Hester were a dog he had taken for a walk. Once inside, Martin sat her at the table for a breakfast of watery oatmeal and a single cup of water before instructing her to lay down on the bed once more. After tying her wrists and ankles, Martin sat back, regarding her half-naked form. The chemise, paltry protection at best, had ridden up her thighs.

"I'm chilled." Hester nodded to the moth-eaten blanket.

Martin didn't immediately respond. Instead, his gaze traveled up her body, far too long at the apex of her thighs. "Lovely copper hair," he whispered. "Everywhere."

Hester tried to pull her legs together, but the rope prohibited it.

The *only* bright spot in this horrible situation had been Martin's admonition that he wouldn't force himself on her, but his depraved morals apparently decided studying her exposed form was perfectly acceptable. Mad as a hatter, but still, ridiculously, a gentleman. Physical relations, Martin insisted, would not take place before they were wed. He would not give in to her subtle seduction.

Martin always spoke as if Hester walked about flirting and plying him with sly innuendo.

His hand suddenly descended to cup her breast. Disgust roiled through her as he massaged the small globe, grunting in satisfaction when the nipple grew taut.

"Get your hands off of me." She tried to avoid his touch.

"I think you need a real man in your bed, darling Hester." His gaze stayed focused on her breast.

"Then I suppose you won't do," she unwisely retorted.

Nothing could be gained by Martin becoming incensed.

"I understand," he said quietly. "Why you sought comfort from Sinclair. I was a married man and unable to be with you, though we longed for each other."

The oatmeal pitched in Hester's stomach.

Martin's eye twitched as he continued to toy with her breast. "I forgive you, my sweet Hester."

"How generous."

"First you were wed to the elderly Black, and then I was forced to wed Ellie. The fates conspired to keep us apart but now we finally can be together as we were meant to. You need to be properly bedded. Worshipped." The hand on her breast retreated. "I will not give in to temptation. I won't defile you before you are my wife. I will show you the respect you deserve, my darling Hester."

She turned her head, not wanting to listen to his insane rants any longer. Instead, she closed her eyes and thought of Drew taking her atop the desk in the study at Blackbird Heath. The whisper of him against the skin of her neck as he gently turned her to press a tender kiss on her lips. Once they'd both found their release, he'd held her gently throbbing body in his lap, stroking her hair until the sound of Mrs. Ebersole's steps approaching had her tidying her clothing. Hester had never felt so—*cherished*—in all her life. Safe from the world.

Too late she sensed the warmth crawling over her skin and tried to force the memory away.

"I can see just the thought of the delights we'll share has you blushing," he cooed, sounding pleased. "Don't worry, darling Hester. I'll be gentle." Martin pressed a kiss to the tip of her nose. "Think of the children I'll give you."

Dear God. A child of Martin's. Tied to him forever.

"I won't lie, my darling Hester."

Her temples ached each time he used that sappy endearment.

"I was happy to know Black couldn't get you with child. Everyone in Horncastle knew of his injury. But rest assured, if the impossible had happened, I would have raised it as my own." Martin sat back; chest puffed out as if he'd bestowed some miracle on her. One might almost think him normal, except for the crazed twitching of his left eye.

For the first time, Hester was glad Drew was in London. If he were here, Martin might succeed in killing him.

"Well, as I've said. I have preparations to finish." A triumphant laugh sounded. "I'll finally have you. Til death do we part." Martin pressed a tender kiss to her lips before standing and going to the table where the remnants of her oatmeal still sat in a bowl. "I can see you're anticipating our wedding as much as I. You can barely eat because of your excitement."

Hester turned away from him once more. If she were lucky, he'd fall off his horse or shoot himself with the pistol he carried in his coat. The thought of Martin touching the most intimate parts of her body made Hester physically ill. Perhaps she could find a way to hit him with something while he was—

"Just stop it." Martin suddenly shouted at her, dropping the bowl that had held what was left of the oatmeal. "This instant, Hester."

She looked over at him, heart racing at the scowl on his face and the almost feral look in his eyes. "I don't—"

"Stop thinking about Sinclair." His brows drew together, lips curled into an ugly sneer. "You aren't going to see him again. Ever. He's in London. Probably in bed with another woman at this very moment. Tupping the bloody life out of her. I doubt he even remembers what you look like." He wobbled a bit and smoothed down his coat, before running his fingers through his hair, tugging on the ends. "Look what you've made me do, darling Hester."

She took a shaky breath, staring at the shards of pottery strewn across the cabin floor. One had slid beneath the bed. Hester wasn't sure what good that would do her, considering her wrists and ankles were bound, but he would have to allow her to get dressed at some point. She might have a chance to grab that shard.

"I'm sorry, Martin. Truly. I apologize. I'm not thinking about Sinclair. I promise. I'm deciding whether the stain on the ceiling..." she tilted her chin with a smile. "Looks like a dog."

He closed his eyes, but she could still see the twitching of his left. The tremor moved along his temple and cheek. "Yes," he took a deep breath, and blinked. "A dog. I agree. See how well we get along. Much better than me and Ellie. When she toppled over at tea," he bent to pick up the shards of bowl, "I nearly wept with relief. I do wish she hadn't coughed up blood. The sight ruined the taste of the scone I was eating."

Hester kept a polite smile on her face, struck with horror at his words. The broken pottery was sharp. He could just as easily stab her with it. Her best hope was the piece of the bowl still under the bed. She only had to find a way to reach it, then Hester would have a weapon.

Martin was stronger, mad, and had no reluctance at all about harming anyone in his path.

But Hester was smarter.

Chapter Twenty-Eight

Drew had run out of places to look for Hester, becoming more frantic as the day wore on. Though Dobbins had already inquired at Martin Godwick's house and been informed Mr. Godwick was not in town at present, Drew decided to venture to the solicitor's office one more time in hopes of catching Godwick unawares. Reaching the office, he peered through the darkened windows, relieved to see a shadow moving about in the far corner of the room.

He knocked. Loudly.

Godwick's clerk, a spare little man named Stone who Drew had met on his previous visit, came to the door. "Mr. Godwick," Stone's muted voice came through the window, "is not in. Godwick & Sons is closed."

"But I need a copy of the contract he prepared for me," Drew blurted out. "Mr. Godwick informed me he'd left a copy in his office, I had only to stop by and retrieve it. Please, it is of the utmost importance. Mr. Stone, isn't it? Do you recall we met the last time I was in Horncastle? I'm Mr. Sinclair."

"Mr. Sinclair? Yes, of course." Stone unlocked the door with a shrug. "I suppose it doesn't matter if I allow you to come inside and watch you comb through his desk. Would serve him right. Come in then, I'll find the contract. Mr. Godwick," the words were laced with sarcasm. "Is on holiday."

"Is he? How strange." Drew pretended confusion before bestowing his usual charm on Stone. "Mr. Godwick didn't mention going on holiday to me, but I'm probably not in his confidence as you are. I only just missed him yesterday when he visited Blackbird Heath."

"Blackbird Heath?" Mr. Stone went to Godwick's office door and opened it. "You must be mistaken, Mr. Sinclair. Mr. Godwick is in Lincoln. Or at least that's what he's told me. And everyone else," he muttered under his breath before pulling out a thick file and slapping it on the desk. "Apparently, there is a young lady in Lincoln who he plans to wed." A disapproving scowl pulled at his lips. "A widow. Mrs. Godwick is barely cold in her grave. I find it distasteful, as does all of Horncastle."

Martin Godwick, in addition to the list of other undesirable traits, was apparently a braggart. "A widow in Lincoln?"

"I don't know who she is, Mr. Sinclair, but I must assume Mr. Godwick has been carrying on with her for some time. He's been making inquiries about obtaining a marriage license and not through the usual channels, probably due to the haste with which he wishes to wed. I only know because he had me make some of those inquiries."

Drew knew Godwick had taken Hester, but he hadn't considered the solicitor meant to wed her. And Godwick had laid the trail perfectly. He'd probably already obtained a license and informed anyone he could that he'd be wedding. Hester had left behind a letter stating she was going to Lincoln. Godwick meant to return to Horncastle, legally wed to Hester all the while spouting his nonsense. Once they were wed, there was little Drew could do.

I can make her a widow again.

Drew pasted a pleasant smile on his face once more. "I can understand his discretion."

"Mr. *Mason* Godwick, Senior," the clerk paused, "may he rest in peace, would be *horrified* by his son's behavior. As am I." A sigh escaped Stone. "It is just as well I will no longer be in his employ."

Drew regarded the clerk with sympathy. "I am sorry to hear that,

Mr. Stone. I found you to be a most competent clerk."

"Thank you, Mr. Sinclair." Stone gave a sniff. "My loyalty has always been to the elder Mr. Godwick. He'd asked me many times to watch out for his son, who was unwell at times."

Clearly, Godwick's father had found something amiss with his son.

"It is the only reason I've stayed on since Mr. Godwick's death despite his son threatening to fire me at every turn." He looked up at Drew. "It was I who sent the letter informing you of Blackbird Heath. I'm sorry it took me so long to find it."

Because Martin had intentionally hidden the documents. Drew might still be unaware of his ownership of the estate had Stone not found and sent the letter.

He strolled about the office, noting the small miniature of a lovely blonde dressed in pale blue. "Mrs. Godwick, I take it."

"Yes." Stone flushed a bit. "Gone far too soon." He cast a glance at the miniature, his pudgy face worshipful.

Interesting. It seemed Martin Godwick wasn't the only one suffering from unrequited love. Perhaps Drew could use that to his advantage.

"Mrs. Godwick was quite lovely. From my brief time in Horncastle, I heard her mentioned with great respect."

"Everyone loved her."

Drew moved from the portrait of Ellie Godwick to a drawing of a small house next to a stream, tucked into the woods. A hunting lodge of sorts, perhaps. The artist had been quite good.

"This is a lovely drawing," Drew said, feeling a hum beneath his skin. "A hunting cottage of Mr. Godwick's? I don't recall seeing it on my travels around Horncastle."

Stone opened up the folder, leafing through the documents before looking up. "Not a hunting lodge, it's not nearly so fine. More a place to fish. Mason Godwick loved to fish. Trout, mostly. He took me there for a few days once. We fished. Drank a great deal of brandy. Unusual, to be sure, for a solicitor and his clerk. But we were quite close." He frowned. "Pity his son never cared for the place. I'm sure it's fallen into disrepair."

Drew's heart thumped harder in his chest as he stared at the drawing. Godwick would want to keep Hester somewhere near Horncastle but secluded. "Is it nearby?"

"In a manner of speaking. The area is remote. Well off any known road. Mr. Godwick said the trout didn't care for noise. And he liked the silence."

Hester was there. Drew would bet his life on it. "Stone, do you recall where this cabin is located?"

"I do. As I said, I've been there several times. Not only to fish, of course. That was only the one time. But I used to take Mr. Godwick papers and such when he was there."

"Can you draw me a map? Give me directions?"

"Of course, but—" The clerk's brow furrowed.

"And Stone, I'm going to need you to do the same for the constable when you alert him immediately after I depart."

Chapter Twenty-Nine

Drew urged his horse faster, glancing down every so often at the map clasped in one hand, grateful that Stone detested Martin Godwick and had been only too happy to help once Drew explained some of the situation and swore the clerk to secrecy. At least until Hester was safe. Godwick was clearly not in his right mind and there wasn't any telling what he was capable of.

Hester, I'm coming.

He cursed himself again for leaving her to the tender mercy of Godwick, and for doubting her.

Stone clearly detested Martin Godwick and relayed a wealth of information about his soon-to-be former employer. Godwick, according to Stone, had been behaving oddly for some time. Stone had witnessed several violent episodes recently, one in which Godwick had repeatedly punched a wall until his hand was a mass of bruises and blood. The elder Mr. Godwick harbored suspicions about his son, but it wasn't until after Martin wed Ellie that he confided in Stone. The clerk also mentioned the sudden death of the elder Godwick from a fall down a flight of stairs in which he'd hit his head. But before that, Martin's father had complained of a stomach ailment to Stone, the same as Ellie Godwick.

There was also the matter of a strange man who'd come to Godwick & Son's only last week. Stone didn't hear the man's name, but he'd barged in and argued with Godwick about payment before storming out, cradling the splint wrapped around his obviously broken wrist.

Drew's assailant in Horncastle. Hired by Godwick.

Stone said Ellie Godwick had hurled numerous accusations at her husband over his attentions to Joshua Black's widow. The clerk overheard one argument that had sent Mrs. Godwick weeping from her husband's office.

"Tell the constable everything," Drew commanded the clerk before riding off. "All your suspicions."

The road became narrower, now little more than a path, just as Stone had warned him. Slowing his horse, Drew looked down and saw fresh hoofprints.

He had not been wrong. Hester was here.

The sound of a bubbling stream met his ears, somewhere to the left, though Drew couldn't see the water. Finally, the line of trees broke into a small clearing, He could just make out the roof of a structure disappearing into the forest. Leading his horse around the other side of the path, he tied up the animal, leaving it to graze in a meadow far enough away from the cabin so as not to be seen.

Drew snuck along the edges of the path, careful not to make a sound. He had no weapon on him save a knife, which would do him little good unless he got close enough to Godwick. He'd been in such a hurry to return to Blackbird Heath, he'd left his pistol in London and Hester only owned an ancient hunting rifle which would probably backfire and injure whoever used it.

The cabin appeared deserted. No horse was tied out outside. He watched for a good fifteen minutes before cautiously approaching, half expecting an enraged Godwick to come barreling out with a pistol, but nothing happened. Making his way up the steps to the cabin, he winced as the ancient wood of the porch creaked beneath his feet, before he flattened against the wall.

HESTER FROZE ON the bed. Someone was standing on the porch. She held her breath, expecting Martin but the door stayed shut. Keeping one eye on the front of the cabin, she took a breath and strained once more to grab the shard of pottery just lying out of reach.

She had managed to get one ankle free. Martin hadn't tied that foot as tightly as the knots holding her wrists or other leg. Hester had thrown one leg over the side of the bed, kicking off the blanket while she tried desperately to grab at the shard of pottery with her toes. After what felt like hours, she'd finally managed to push it closer with the edge of her foot. The problem, of course, was what she would do once she got hold of it.

"One thing at a time, Hester," she muttered to herself.

If she could get the shard on the bed and she couldn't manage to loosen one of her wrists, then she would hide it beneath her body. When Martin untied her tonight to see to her needs, Hester would grab the shard and stab Martin in the neck.

A breath left her at the thought.

She didn't want to kill Martin, but there was no other way to escape him. And Hester would only get one chance. Her toes finally curled around the shard and she carefully lifted her foot to the bed, twisting her leg—

A shadow flashed by the window.

No. No. No. Martin couldn't be back so soon.

Hester dropped the piece of pottery as close to her body as she could, sliding her hip over the top to hide it, her heart racing in her chest at the thought of what she must do.

DREW STOOD ALONGSIDE the wall of the cabin, beside the door, ear pressed to the rotting wood, listening for any sound. If Godwick was inside, he hadn't noticed Drew's arrival, or worse, he wasn't here. Which meant Hester wasn't either and he was too late.

Though he wasn't stupid enough to put himself directly in front of the door, Drew had peeked through a tiny window to his right, the glass was so dirty he couldn't see anything.

Malcolm, his brother, was skilled at a variety of nefarious things. He'd be pleased Drew had actually listened when at his instructions on how to properly storm a building. But Mal would also have smacked Drew in the head for being so stupid as to face Godwick and rescue Hester with only a knife.

I should have asked Stone if there was a pistol in Godwick's office.

Far too late now. At least he was assured the constable would be summoned, but he had no idea how long it would take him to arrive. And if Hester wasn't inside—

Fear curdled his stomach. Godwick might already have spirited her away. For all he knew, Hester was Godwick's wife by now. Not willingly. He refused to believe the tiny bit of doubt that pricked at him, whispering he'd driven Hester into Godwick's waiting arms.

Or that once safe, Hester would not want Drew either.

He cracked open the door an inch. When nothing was hurled at him or a shot wasn't fired, Drew stepped inside the one room cabin. Barely any light shone from the lone window, and he squinted into the murky interior. He caught sight of a table on the far side of the room, where a discarded apple core sat beside a shattered bowl. A bed sat in the corner. The blankets piled atop shifted as he entered.

"Drew," a familiar voice sobbed. "My God. Drew."

"Hester." Drew rushed to the bed. "What has he done to you?" The bastard had tied her to the bed. Pulling the knife from his pocket, he searched for any sign of injury. "Did he hurt you?"

Cupping her chin with one hand, he closed his eyes, and pressed a kiss to her forehead, thanking whatever unknown force had compelled him to depart London with such haste. "I knew something was wrong. I felt it."

"Hurry," she whispered, her voice breaking. "Martin will return soon. He's mad, Drew. He tried to kill you. It wasn't me. I would never—"

"I figured that part out. Eventually. I'm a complete half-wit, Hester. I should have known—"

"Andrew Sinclair," she said in her usual no nonsense tone. "You can admit to me what a bloody idiot you are *after* we are gone from here. Martin might arrive at any moment." A ragged sound came from Hester, her body trembling beneath his fingers. "Hurry."

Drew slashed through her binding with the knife. "Stupid of me to accuse you. To argue about it. You never would have wasted the coin required to hire an assassin. Not when there is fertilizer to purchase, and animals to feed. You're far too practical and frugal." He leaned over to cut through the rope still binding one of her ankles. "You were more likely to have Mrs. Ebersole poison me. That's what I determined."

Freed, Hester threw herself into his arms. "You are correct on both points. But more importantly, I don't want to be rid of you." Her eyes filled with tears. "Ever."

Drew pulled her into his arms. "I know."

"You are what matters most to me." Hester pressed her nose into his chest. "Far more than Blackbird Heath. I should have told you." Another tiny sob left her. "But you made me so bloody angry, Drew. Thinking I could—I assumed you were only using it as an excuse to leave me. I'm no Lady Downing."

No, Hester would never be Constance and Drew was grateful for it.

"I will never leave you, Hester Black," he whispered into her hair, meaning every word. "Not ever. But let us discuss my stupidity and our stubborn natures in the comfort of our own bed once we are home. The constable is on his way, but I don't want to encounter Martin Godwick. Not when all I have is this blade." He slid the knife back into his pocket.

Hester nodded and lifted her head. "He's truly mad, Drew. Obsessed with me and I've no idea why. He believes us to be star-crossed lovers." She gave him an urgent look. "Martin killed his wife. And his father."

After speaking to Mr. Stone and hearing his suspicions, Drew was not surprised at the revelation. "We should go." He came to his feet and took Hester's hand.

The door to the cabin flew open, one of the boards falling free and toppling to the floor.

"Well, well." A disheveled, and frenzied looking, Martin Godwick stood in the doorway. His eyes were wild as he took in the two of them, mouth jerking about as he spoke. Disheveled, coat buttoned incorrectly, Martin advanced on them.

Drew barely recognized him.

Where is the constable? He dropped Hester's hand and felt for the reassurance of the knife in his coat. Not that it would do much good. Godwick had a pistol clutched in one twitching hand. One slip of the finger and the thing might go off.

"If it isn't Andrew Sinclair." Godwick's arm came up, shaking and unsteady, to aim the weapon directly at Drew's chest. "I can't possibly miss this time."

Chapter Thirty

Hester stared in horror at Martin for less than a minute before wiping her features clean of any emotion. He must not see her fear or disappointment at his appearance. Nothing must be said or done to set him off, not when he had a pistol pointed at Drew's chest. Martin's hair stood on end, left eye twitching so violently he appeared to be winking at her.

Whatever was *wrong* with Martin, was getting worse.

"I can't believe I missed you on the road from Horncastle." Martin's entire body made an odd jerking motion as if he weren't completely in control of his limbs.

"The Sinclairs are tough to be rid of," Drew replied, sliding away from Hester as Martin's pistol followed the movement. "Just ask Lady Longwood. She's compared us to ants who infest the flour in one's pantry." He was trying to protect her by moving away, ensuring that Martin wouldn't accidentally shoot her.

"At this short distance, I'm unlikely to miss," Martin snarled at Drew, before finally sparing a glance at Hester. "How could you? We are to be married tomorrow, Hester. I've bought a dress. A ring. Found a vicar who has few objections." He waved the pistol about, fingers jerking over the trigger. "*We* are supposed to be together, darling Hester."

"And we will be, dear Martin." It was all she could do to get her mouth to form the words, but they had the desired effect. Martin was focused completely on her.

Hester stepped carefully in her captor's direction, ignoring Drew's panicked look. "He," she pointed at Drew, "stormed in here. I tried to tell him that I was in no need of his assistance. Dear Martin," she implored. "Why would I want some," the words thickened with emotion, "some gambling wastrel? I told Sinclair to go away."

Confusion darted across Martin's features, already contorted by the force of whatever fanatical notions gripped him. He no longer looked like the dashing, handsome solicitor of Horncastle, but instead, something monstrous and terrible.

"You told him to leave?" he whined. "For us?"

"Your affection for me—well, it was frightening at first. But now I realize that you have been right all along. We are meant to be together." Hester smiled, hoping Drew understood what she was trying to do.

"But Hester." Drew gave her an anguished look. He placed a hand over his heart. "I thought—"

"I only wanted you to give me Blackbird Heath," she sneered, making sure to keep her gaze firmly fixed on Martin. "Not you. But now that you've given it to me, I've no further use for you, Mr. Sinclair. Our relationship is at an end." Hester said exactly what Martin wanted to hear most and she prayed it would be enough to convince him.

"I did so much for you, darling Hester," Martin choked. "My father nearly ruined all my plans by forcing me to marry Ellie. I never would have sent for him," he jerked his chin in Drew's direction. "That was my father's doing and Stone's. But I fixed all of that. For us." His head shook as if something were lodged in his ears. "Well, except for Stone."

"You are so brave, my dearest. You've done so much for me. And now we have Blackbird Heath. I promise not to give you cause to sell it. I want nothing more than to be your wife, Martin."

The twitching of Martin's eye became that much worse, the lid nearly closing completely. The hand clutching the pistol trembled and lowered.

"Hester. My darling Hester." Tears ran down his cheeks. "Finally, you understand."

"I do," she said, as Drew rushed past her and slammed into Martin, knocking him to the floor. Drew had grown up with two brothers and knew how to throw a punch, but Martin fought like a wild animal, gnashing his teeth and making the most horrible noises.

The two wrestled across the floor, each struggling to gain control of the pistol. She'd hoped Drew could draw the blade in his coat, but he had no opportunity. Hester grabbed the shard of pottery off the bed, meaning to stab Martin with it when Drew hit him in the temple, twice. The pistol finally fell from Martin's fingers and skidded across the floor.

He growled, rolling over with inhuman strength. He grabbed Drew and wrapped his fingers around his throat.

Drew desperately tried to throw Martin off.

Hester jumped to the side and grabbed the pistol. She'd never fired one, but she could handle a rifle. It couldn't possibly be that much different. "Get off him," she said, pointing the pistol directly at Martin. "Now."

"Hester, my darling," Martin implored her, his fingers loosened their hold but were still wrapped around Drew's neck. "What are you doing? Shoot the bugger. I'll burn the cabin. No one will ever find the body. We can be wed tonight. In Lincoln. I have the license."

Drew came up on his shoulders and butted his skull into Martin's nose.

Martin shrieked, blood pouring from his nose. "Hester. Darling Hester."

"I told you I grew up with two brothers," Drew snapped before twisting away and kicking Martin in the chin with the heel of his boot.

"Stay put."

"No." Martin tore at his hair, hands covered in blood and attempted to get to his feet.

Drew kicked him again.

"Hester, what are you doing?" Martin sobbed, snot and blood pouring down his chin. "You love me." He banged his hand against the floor like a toddler having a tantrum. He shot Drew a murderous look, left eye twitching along with one side of his mouth.

"May I?" Drew plucked the pistol from Hester's shaking fingers. "Though I find the sight of you wielding a pistol to be highly erotic, it would be best if I handled this part. I'm quite good with a pistol." He looked at the slobbering mess of Martin on the floor. "Much better than you, Godwick. The way you were waving it about, you were just as likely to shoot yourself. If you don't stop whining I'll shoot the tips of your ears off."

Martin jerked back.

"Or a finger. Perhaps your knees—or something else." The pistol hovered below Martin's waist.

"Drew," Hester cautioned. "Please do not." She glanced at Martin who had fallen to the floor and was spinning himself about with one foot while holding his broken nose. "What do we do now?"

"We wait." Drew's gaze and the pistol never moved from Martin. "Mr. Stone doesn't care for you at all, Godwick. I had a lovely chat with him earlier today, which is how I found this cabin. He also sent for the constable, who I expect at any moment."

Hester *had* wondered how Drew came to find her. She'd forgotten all about Martin's clerk, Mr. Stone.

"Stone's a terrible clerk. I should have fired him after he forwarded my father's letter to you, Sinclair." He jerked towards Hester but stopped at the sound of the pistol cocking.

"I really do want to shoot you, Godwick." Drew's voice simmered with rage. "So please, keep moving about."

Martin pounded the floor again with his fist as the sound of horses approaching filtered into the cabin. "Darling Hester." He leapt in her direction.

The sound of the pistol firing stopped him.

"I did warn you," Drew said casually.

Martin squealed in pain, clutching his foot. "I'll kill you."

"I doubt it. Those horses undoubtedly belong to the constable. You should wrap your cravat around your foot to stop the bleeding."

"I trusted you, Hester," Martin sobbed as the chief constable and two others, including Mr. Stone, came through the door, their own weapons drawn. "Arrest this man. I'm Martin Godwick. He shot me in the foot."

The constable looked at Drew. "I know who you are, Mr. Godwick."

Drew lowered his pistol and quickly grabbed the blanket from the bed to cover her. She'd completely forgotten she had on only a chemise. He explained what had happened in the cabin and what Godwick had done and planned to do.

"Mr. Stone has filled me in, Mr. Sinclair." The two other men with the constable picked Martin off the floor. "We'll take care of Mr. Godwick."

"Murderer," Mr. Stone hissed at Martin as he followed the men out.

Once the constable took Martin away, Hester's legs started to shake. She sat down on the bed, unable to stop trembling. She'd been so afraid that her solicitor and his plans would succeed right up until the moment he was taken away.

"Hester." Drew slipped an arm around her. "It's over, love. I promise."

She was not the sort of woman who dissolved into fits of weeping. Or fainted. Wailed. Carried on. It wasn't in her nature. But enclosed in Drew's arms, with his scent in her nostrils, a horrific sob came from her. She clutched at Drew's coat, clinging to him as if she were a terrified child.

"He threatened to kill Mrs. Ebersole. Mary. Her sister had an accident," she wept. "Martin caused it. How could I have not known he was dangerous?" She looked up at him, tears running down her cheeks. "I never encouraged him. Never, Drew."

"No one guessed that Godwick was capable of such things. His father worried over his son's behavior, as did Mr. Stone. But kidnapping? Murder?" Drew shook his head. "And as to his fixation on you—I can't explain it. You cannot blame yourself, Hester. And I promise, he won't hurt you or anyone else at Blackbird Heath."

"You can't promise that." She sniffed.

"I can. I'm not leaving you. And I'm certain Godwick will never be free again to roam about."

Hester's heart swelled with hope. Yes, he'd rescued her. Apologized for his accusations. But Drew's life was still in London, far from here. "You don't like cabbage," she murmured. "Or the country."

"It was the only thing that grew at Dunnings, and I will always detest it." Drew gave a little shiver. "Terrible, noxious odor. Only good for feeding the pigs."

"But there's Mr. Worthington and your partnership," she protested. "You can't—give that up for me and Blackbird Heath."

"Oh, I won't." He kissed her gently. We will compromise, Mrs. Black. Live at Blackbird Heath and pay visits to London. That is, if you'll have me."

Hester nodded, sobbing louder as she pressed her face into Drew's coat. "I'll have you, you dandified charlatan."

Drew chuckled, stroking her hair. "Exactly the sort of response I expected. I love you too."

Epilogue

L ONDON WAS A terrifying experience.
Full of people, horses, and carriages of every size. Soot hanging in the air belched by factories Hester could only glimpse in the distance. The noise alone was deafening.

She took Drew's hand, clasping his fingers.

Hester had never been further than Horncastle her entire life, or wished to ever leave Lincolnshire. But Drew had asked for a compromise and since Hester could no longer imagine her life without him, she agreed.

After what happened in the cabin, Drew had only left Hester's side once, to return briefly to London for his sister's wedding. Hester stayed behind, at her insistence. She was perfectly safe.

Martin Godwick had been committed to the Middlesex County Lunatic Asylum at Hanwell outside of London and would no longer be a threat to himself or anyone else. And, she reasoned with Drew, she couldn't leave Blackbird Heath, not while there were crops, animals and the bees, requiring her attention. Reluctantly, he departed for London without her and stayed away only a week.

It felt to Hester like a lifetime.

Compromise, she acknowledged, was the key to a lasting relationship. Now it was her turn.

Mrs. Ebersole had helped Hester pack for their journey, exclaiming over the half-dozen new gowns Drew had purchased for her on their recent trip to Grantham. She'd protested the expense, but now, seeing the richly garbed ladies as their carriage rolled down the street, Hester was glad she'd allowed Drew to win that argument. Also, as he'd cheerily mentioned one morning as his mouth descended to tease one of her nipples, he was disgustingly wealthy.

Hester looked down at her gloved fingers, clasped tightly to Drew's. The balm she'd purchased in Grantham had improved the appearance of her hands, but they would never be those of a lady. And Drew didn't seem to mind.

"Don't be nervous," he pressed his lips to the inside of her wrist. "None of them bite." He tilted his chin. "At least not much."

Compromise, Hester reminded herself, mainly to keep from leaping out of the carriage and running back to Lincolnshire.

"Ah, we're here." The carriage rolled to a stop before a stately home.

Hester's eyes widened as she took in the Sinclair London residence. Blackbird Heath was no more than a pauper's cottage compared to Emerson House.

Drew jumped out, holding out his hand as two footmen hurried down the steps, followed by a man who reminded Hester oddly of a mastiff.

"Good afternoon, Holly." Drew greeted the giant.

"Mr. Sinclair," he bowed, regarding Hester with curiosity. "The family awaits you in the drawing room." He waved them forward. "They received your letter."

"Splendid."

Hester sat frozen in the carriage. "I'll just wait here."

"Will you be sleeping here as well? I believe there is a perfectly comfortable bed upstairs just for us." He winked. "Stop stalling."

She nodded and took Drew's hand, allowing herself to be led up the steps, hearing the soft rustle of her blue and white striped silk skirts. Such finery took time to get accustomed to, but she did like her traveling outfit.

"Holly's the butler," Drew whispered to her, taking the opportunity to nip at the skin beneath her ear. "I believe he was once a criminal. I don't recall. Tamsin found him."

Her foot faltered as she went up the steps, and Hester had the urge to simply dig in her heels and refuse to go further.

"Don't be stubborn," Drew said under his breath.

"I'm not."

"You were the other evening. Refusing to acknowledge the column you added incorrectly in the ledger. We are running a farm. You must pay attention."

Hester's cheeks stung as she blushed furiously at his comment.

She and Drew disagreed over the way the accounting was handled for Blackbird Heath mainly because Drew was always correct, and Hester didn't care to admit it. The argument always ended with Hester spread out across the desk in the study, skirts tossed up, while Drew did—

Her face burned.

An *assortment* of things to her. All highly pleasurable. Hester had started intentionally making mistakes in the ledgers. Pretending she didn't know how much feed she'd purchased. Or what the price was of a jar of honey.

Holly ushered them to the drawing room, opening the door with a bow.

Hester took a deep breath and took in the group of people scattered about the gorgeous room. The stunning woman seated on the settee, a glass of what must be Irish whiskey, dangling from her hand, must be Tamsin. She would have known Drew's sister even if Tamsin didn't look so much like her brother, because an overly large gentleman with blades of grass stuck on the sleeve of his coat hovered protectively over her slender form.

The Duke of Ware.

The handsome gentleman dressed expensively in a finely tailored coat had to be the Earl of Emerson, though he had no hint of Drew's graceful elegance. Lord Emerson looked more like the men who used to brawl with her father in Horncastle's taverns.

The woman by his side was Odessa, Lady Emerson. There was a slight, elderly woman seated on a chair in the corner, discreetly sipping on brandy. Miss Maplehurst was exactly as Drew had described her. And the lovely young woman dressed in pink silk, Aurora.

Hester took a deep breath. Drew had said, repeatedly, that she had nothing to fear from the Sinclairs. His family subsisted on the very edge of society and were considered somewhat scandalous, no matter that they now counted a duke and duchess among them.

If Tamsin possessed any real manners, Drew said he'd yet to see it. Ware collected insects. Odessa made wax masks of everyone's face and told gruesome stories over the dinner table. Jordan raised pigs. And he despaired of his young sister Aurora with the flirtatious Miss Maplehurst as her chaperone.

The only one missing was Malcolm Sinclair, Drew's twin brother. But Hester's understanding was that he would arrive shortly for Aurora's official debut. He was a mercenary. At least, Drew thought that's what he did, now that Malcolm was no longer a soldier.

Hester had been promised she would be the *least* odd person in attendance.

"Finally," Tamsin sailed towards them, her eyes alight with curiosity. "You're late as usual, Drew. I suppose you had to stop in every window between here and Lincolnshire to check your reflection."

"Not once, dear sister." Drew kissed Tamsin's cheek. "And I'm sorry we're late. We had a stop to make before reaching London. One of the utmost importance."

"A game of whist doesn't count."

Drew pretended a great deal of mock outrage. "This was much more important than a game of cards." He turned to Hester, love shining from his eyes. "We had to stop for a wedding."

Lord Emerson nudged his wife in the ribs. "I told you," he said softly.

Drew took Hester's hand and pulled her close. "I'd like to introduce you all to my wife, Hester."

About the Author

Kathleen Ayers is the bestselling author of steamy Regency and Victorian romance. She's been a hopeful romantic and romance reader since buying Sweet Savage Love at a garage sale when she was fourteen while her mother was busy looking at antique animal planters. She has a weakness for tortured, witty alpha males who can't help falling for intelligent, sassy heroines.

A Texas transplant (from Pennsylvania) Kathleen spends most of her summers attempting to grow tomatoes (a wasted effort) and floating in her backyard pool with her two dogs, husband and son. When not writing she likes to visit her "happy place" (Newport, RI.), wine bars, make homemade pizza on the grill, and perfect her charcuterie board skills. Visit her at www.kathleenayers.com.

Printed in Great Britain
by Amazon